"I'm Not a Fool, Mr. Alexander!"

"I like a girl with spirit," Louis Alexander
said, but he said it arrogantly, as though he
knew he could break that spirit if and when
he chose. He took Rosalie's hands and raised
them to his lips. As his lips touched her
fingers a fire went right through her and,
frightened, she jerked her hands away. She
must not forget why she was here. Not for the
job. Not for the money. Rosalie was here for
revenge.

JADE WALTERS
makes her home in a quaint, old-fashioned
English village, but her lifetime hobby has been
seeing the world. She and her husband have
traveled from the islands of Greece to the
mountains of the Himalayas, and their real-life
experiences have often formed the background
for one of this prolific author's many stories.

D0522887

Dear Reader:

I'd like to take this opportunity to thank you for all your support and encouragement of Silhouette Romances.

Many of you write in regularly, telling us what you like best about Silhouette, which authors are your favorites. This is a tremendous help to us as we strive to publish the best contemporary romances possible.

All the romances from Silhouette Books are for you, so enjoy this book and the many stories to come. I hope you'll continue to share your thoughts with us, and invite you to write to us at the address below:

Editor-in-Chief,
Silhouette Books,
P.O. Box 910,
517 Lorne Ave.,
Stratford, Ontario N5A 6W3

JADE WALTERS
Greek Idyll

Silhouette *Romance*

Published by Silhouette Books New York

Distributed in Canada by PaperJacks Ltd., a Licensee
of the trademarks of Simon & Schuster, a division of
Gulf+Western Corporation.

SILHOUETTE BOOKS, a Simon & Schuster Division of
GULF & WESTERN CORPORATION
1230 Avenue of the Americas, New York, N.Y. 10020
In Canada distributed by PaperJacks Ltd.,
330 Steelcase Road, Markham, Ontario.

ISBN: 0-671-57211-3

First Silhouette Books printing March, 1983

10 9 8 7 6 5 4 3 2 1

Map by Ray Lundgren

Printed in Canada

To Wal

Greek
Idyll

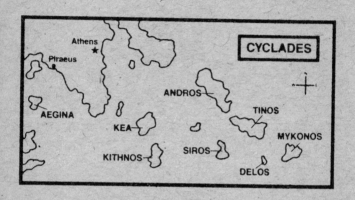

Chapter One

The sun had already gone down and a pearly mist lay over the Berkshire countryside. The giant oaks and chestnuts were heavy with summer leaf. Beneath the one on the very edge of the graveyard a small gray squirrel sat up on his haunches licking his tiny paws. Rosalie was about to step through the lich gate when someone emerged from the gate that led into the lane, a tall, masculine figure moving with an air of arrogance in his bearing and a lithe stride. He went directly along the path between the gravestones, then without hesitation swung off and waded through the long, untidy grass. Toward the grave? Yes, for suddenly he saw the banked flowers and quickened his step. He stood beside them for a moment, hands behind his back, looking down, his head bent low. Then Rosalie saw him kneel and place something on the ground.

Puzzled, she moved forward. He must have heard

her footstep crunching on the gravel, for he glanced up; then, with head bowed as though in obeisance, he faced the grave again momentarily before turning on his heel to return swiftly the way he had come. Walking like a leopard, she thought, the powerful muscles hidden by his tailored suit lending an extraordinary animal grace to his movements. Then there was the sound of a door banging in the evening stillness, the roar of an engine, and a long, low sports car came swishing down the lane and raged off into the distance.

Rosalie stood looking after him, anger mounting up in her, for who could the man be but the villainous Louis Alexander, father of Fay's child, who had cold-bloodedly refused to marry her and thereby ruined two lives? Cost two lives, in fact, and ruined another, for Fay and the child had both died and Fay's decent young husband had been left brokenhearted, embittered, and surrounded by the shreds of what had been a good life.

How dare the man come like this, skulking into the darkening churchyard after the funeral was over and everyone gone home! She went angrily along the path between scented flowers toward the grave to which her grandmother had sent her to clip the loving messages from the wreaths. As she came up her eyes raked the mound and were drawn mesmerically, not to a vast, showy wreath as she would have expected, but to a simple little posy of garden flowers—cornflowers and phlox and sweet-smelling lavender. She lifted it up, her hands trembling. She wished she had the nerve to throw it away. There was a plain card attached, and on it was written, poignantly, one word: *Forgiveness.*

Forgiveness? She stared down at that word in angry disbelief. Surely the man did not mean—but he couldn't possibly. That in death Fay should forgive him? The crude, selfish insensibility of the man! Yet had there been something more to their relationship than the family knew? Now that she had seen the man, seen the way he came, quietly, in the reaches of the evening when no one would see him, how he bent his head, almost reverently, over his lover's grave, she began to wonder. And then rage surged up in her when she realized that if it had not been for him Fay would be alive today.

"She seems almost to have a death wish," the doctor had told Rosalie and her grandmother worriedly as the pregnancy dragged on and Fay grew more and more despondent, more and more ill. "It seems to be psychosomatic. I can't find anything really wrong with her." And then suddenly it seemed that the baby was dead, and Fay did not care about going on living. They took the child from her, and after that she only lingered a few more days.

Rosalie walked back up the twisting path beneath the trees, her feet rustling in the carpet of last year's autumn leaves, small birds twittering sleepily in the branches overhead as they settled for the night. The Elizabethan cottage where Rosalie and Fay had been brought up and where their grandmother now lived alone snuggled, mellowed and beautiful, among the big oaks and chestnuts as though it too grew out of the ground that had given them birth. In the evenings when the sun went down it lit up the hanging tiles that decorated the upper part of the house, burnishing them so that they glowed with the warmth of the ruddy conkers that fell from the chestnut trees in autumn.

When the big house had had to be sold on the death of Rosalie's father she and her mother had moved to one of three farmworkers' cottages on the estate.

Then, when Rosalie was two years old, her mother had married Fay's father and he had bought the cottages on either side. The three of them had converted easily and prettily into a delightful house. Rosalie's stepfather, Fay's father, had spent a great deal of money on modernizing the old place, and he had bought some land from the estate when it was sold to enlarge the garden.

Once inside, Rosalie took the card out of her pocket and looked down at it again as she dropped those that had come from the wreaths onto the coffee table. "What's that?" asked her grandmother curiously. She was a tiny woman, shrunken with age, with fine, luxuriant white hair framing a delicately lined face and enhancing her china-blue eyes. She leaned back in the creaking old rocking chair that had been in the family for generations and was her favorite seat.

Rosalie looked at her grandmother appraisingly, wondering whether or not to tell. But she had to tell someone. "It's from Louis Alexander," she said.

"Louis Alexander!" her grandmother exclaimed sharply. "He wasn't at the funeral." Rosalie told her how she had seen the man come into the churchyard and as swiftly make his exit. "Fay used to talk a lot about him in the beginning," said the old lady, "but she never brought him here. Once she showed me a photo. Oh, but what a handsome young man he was! Tall, with dark hair lying across his forehead, and the most beautiful smile I ever saw. Like a film star, I thought he was. I suppose he had all the girls after him and could pick and choose. Perhaps our little Fay wasn't good enough," she ended, gazing misty-eyed into space.

"Not good enough!" Rosalie echoed indignantly. Loving Fay, she refused to accept that the other girl was less than perfect.

12

"Not for a man like him with such a wide choice," her grandmother replied soothingly. "I understand he's very rich. Jets all over the place. He owns a travel business, you know. That's how Fay met him."

"Then he probably jets around at a reduced rate," snapped Rosalie, and her grandmother looked at her with compassion. "Tell me about him."

"I know very little. She went to his agency to find out about flights to Nepal because she wanted to join you in Katmandu the time you went on that rather rough bus trip. She thought she'd have Christmas with you, but she wanted to do it the easy way—very sensibly," she added, looking fondly up at the girl who stood before her.

"Who could blame her? My way of travel isn't everyone's cup of tea," Rosalie retorted dryly. "But she never told me this."

"No. There was no need, because when she went to the agency she met Louis and that was the end of going away. She wouldn't have wanted you to be disappointed."

"I would have been," Rosalie agreed. "And how long did the affair last?"

"Six months, perhaps. I forget. Then suddenly she swept in one day and announced she was going to marry Stephen."

Stephen Barrington, a young estate agent in the nearby town of Cataran, who had fallen in love with Rosalie years before. At that time Fay, mischievously spreading her wings, testing her sexuality, had taken him away. Not that she had wanted him. The little affair lasted only a matter of weeks, but there was no going back afterward to Stephen, for there was embarrassment on one side, hurt on the other. Rosalie went abroad to work, returning from time to time between jobs. Nothing, luckily, was spoiled between

13

the two girls. Fay was headstrong, willful, but somehow she was always forgiven.

"I'll admit now you could have knocked me down with a feather," Gran said, "when Fay announced she and Stephen were going to get married."

"You'd have been even more staggered, I expect, if you'd known she was pregnant—and by someone else."

"I'd have stepped in. Of course I'd have stepped in," her grandmother replied. "It was a dreadful thing to do to Stephen."

The young husband had gradually come to realize, as the time for Fay's confinement came inexorably closer too soon, that the child was not his. They had parted, Fay returning to her grandmother's house. Rosalie had returned from Greece to stand by.

"Somehow, Fay was too glamorous for Stephen," the old lady said now. "And besides, I always expected him to marry you."

"That's a backhanded compliment if ever I heard one," said Rosalie, her tone wry. "Am I that dreary?"

The old lady reached out a hand and took Rosalie's in her own. "You're lovely," she said warmly. "Let's be honest. You were always worth two of Fay. But she had a magnetic quality that had a devastating effect on men. You always had your own quiet brand of charm, but really, now that your hair has gone ash-blond from the sun and you have a perpetual suntan, I think you're prettier."

Rosalie put a delicate finger to her grandmother's lips and they looked at each other for a long moment. "Let's not do anything to Fay's memory." It was too late now, in death, to face what they had refused to acknowledge in the other girl's lifetime.

"No. But you saw Louis Alexander? What did you think, dear?"

"How could I tell, in the dusk?"

Yet she had been able to tell. She had needed no more light than there was to see the long, virile limbs of the man, the arrogant way he held his handsome head. What puzzled her then, and still did, was the curious note of humility he struck when he bent that head, the simplicity of the posy he left behind. If she had expected him to send flowers at all, she would have expected a formal florist's bouquet, impersonal, expensive. And *Forgiveness*. The word still bothered her. How could he ask her to forgive him when, as Fay said, he had had his way with her, then refused to marry her?

She said abruptly, "I'm going to see him."

"Oh, I wouldn't do that, dear," the old lady cautioned hastily. "Not in your present upset state. Not at all, in fact. What's done is done, my darling. There's no bringing Fay back." She patted her white hair nervously. "I'll make a nice cup of tea for us both, then take myself off to bed. It's been a harrowing day, and I'm not as young as I used to be. Will you stay with me a few days before you return to Greece? I can't imagine why you want to spend so much time in those foreign countries, but"—she smiled lovingly up at her tall, slender granddaughter—"if you must, you must."

"Of course I'll stay for a few days," Rosalie replied warmly, "and be glad to. You go to bed, Gran, and I'll get the tea for you."

While her grandmother was preparing for bed in the cozy, chintz-curtained bedroom with its fluffy white carpet, Rosalie picked up the London telephone directory. So, Louis Alexander was in the travel business. She flicked through the pages. Alexander & Radcliff? Could that be him? She took a pencil from the desk and wrote down the address. When the kettle boiled she made tea in the little Georgian silver teapot that had been handed down through the family from generation to generation, set it on a tray with the fine bone china, her grandmother's favorite set with the little pink rosebuds. What was she going to do with that address? Already, in the further reaches of her mind, she knew, but she did not intend to upset her grandmother by telling her.

Carefully she carried the tray up the twisting oak staircase. She put it down on the bedside table, poured the tea, then settled herself on the end of her grandmother's bed. Now that Fay had gone the old lady was going to miss both girls badly, but "You've got your own lives to live," she always said selflessly, "and you know where to find me when you need me."

Afterward, Rosalie lay in bed in her old room staring up at the rough-hewn oak beams of the ceiling and listening to the rustle of the drooping laburnum as it moved to and fro across the tiles in the evening breeze. That same breeze wafted the sweet scent of honeysuckle into the room. Forget Louis Alexander, she said to herself. It's all over. Forget him. And yet she could not. Tossing and turning far into the night, listening to the relentless chimes of the church clock pealing the night hours, she told herself over and over again that what had happened was over and done with. As she had said to Stephen, there was no bringing Fay back.

And yet that one word on the card, *Forgiveness,* haunted her. She turned over, shook away the tumbled bedclothes, tucked her head into the soft pillows, and tried to chase the worrying thoughts away. The man himself bothered her, coming as he had in the secret stillness of the evening when everyone else had gone home, walking purposefully, showing not a vestige of shame in his demeanor. . . . Stop it, she adjured herself. Go to sleep. Bother that clock. She put her fingers in her ears. In the silence the image of the man came up even more clearly in her mind's eye.

Yes, she decided in the end. Yes, I have to see him. And then, as though the decision had put her mind at rest, she drifted off to sleep.

On the pretext of going up to town to book her flight to Athens, Rosalie took a train the next morning and then a bus to Oxford Street. She found the firm of Alexander & Radcliff tucked away in a little lane not far from Oxford Circus. It had a narrow door that opened into a large foyer. There were leather sofas and chairs, and rows of pigeonholes holding travel brochures. On the walls were some glorious posters depicting exciting seascapes in sunshiny lands.

A receptionist was talking on the telephone. Then another telephone on her desk rang and the girl looked at it with harassed eyes. "Just a moment, please." She put one receiver down and picked up the other. Then a bell buzzed on her desk. In apparent despair, she put a hand over both mouthpieces and addressed Rosalie. "I'm sorry. It's like a madhouse this morning. But you're the first to arrive. You must be Miss Hampton." She began shuffling frantically among some papers on the desk. "Now, where on earth is my list of applicants?" she muttered to herself before Rosalie could deny that she was Miss Hampton. "Oh, well," the girl sighed distractedly. "Go on in. Mr. Alexander is free now."

Rosalie had opened her mouth to say she was not Miss Hampton and did not have an appointment when suddenly she realized that if Louis Alexander had a long list of people to interview she was unlikely to see him at all today and her journey would be wasted. With a quick smile, she made for the door marked L. Alexander, tapped briskly, and went in.

Yes, it was indeed the man she had seen in the churchyard who sat behind the desk. Black hair, a smooth olive skin, a mouth that was firmly chiseled, beautifully molded, wide, generous almost, and yet oddly hard. His eyes, framed by short, thick black lashes, were tawny gold. He was wearing a navy-blue business suit, beautifully cut, screaming its origins in Savile Row, but its smooth lines failed to hide the essential strength of the man, and a certain animal primitiveness. Leashed power, she thought, her senses jolted. No wonder her stepsister had fallen for him. "I suppose he had all the girls after him," Gran had said, "and could pick and choose." As indeed he could, Rosalie surmised. She had to give herself a shake, remind herself of his villainous black heart.

As he took in the picture of the tall, slender girl with the long silky blond hair and violet eyes he did a double take, seeming momentarily unnerved. Then a mask slid over his face and he said politely, "Please sit down. My receptionist seems a bit harassed this morning. You, I gather"—he broke off, peering at a list of names—"are Miss Hampton?" He lifted his eyes to hers again, and again there was that queer, shaken look as the mask slipped.

"I've come to—" Rosalie began, then stopped, unable to go on. How could she say to this arrogant man that she had come to delve into the meaning of that word *Forgiveness* on his card?

"Yes," he said. "The job. Do please sit down."

With an odd sense of being swept headlong by a powerful tide, Rosalie backed into the chair that stood before his desk.

"I'll be as brief as possible," he began.

"Mr. Alexander—" She leaned forward, hand raised to stop him, but to her dismay he cut her off again.

"There's something I have to tell you before we proceed."

"Mr. Al—"

"Kindly listen to me." He was quick without appearing hurried. Totally in command in a way that would have been ruthless but for the silken sheath that seemed to lie over him, smoothing without softening. "It will save time in the end. What I want to say to you is that the job isn't what was advertised, so you'd save me a lot of time and trouble by hearing me out. The courier who was leaving has decided to stay, and the girls we want now are for quite a different job. I assume you speak Spanish or French. Which one?"

Rosalie jumped to her feet, half laughing, half angry at the way he walked rough-yet-silken-shod, over her. "I could save you a lot of time too, Mr. Alexander, if you would just listen to me."

"Hear me out first. Let's get this bit about the languages straight," he said coolly, looking her up and down as though assessing her curves rather than her intelligence. His eyes lingered audaciously on the swell of her small breasts beneath the thin cotton dress, on her narrow waist and the slender curve of her hips. "Spanish or French, Miss Hampton? In other words, which country were you applying for? Tell me that, and then I'll explain the change of plan."

Rosalie stamped her foot furiously. "I don't speak Spanish and not much Fr—"

"Then what the devil do you speak?" he rapped out angrily. "Why are you wasting my precious time?"

She lifted her small chin and said icily, "Greek, if

19

it's any of your business. And I'm not Miss Hampton. And I didn't come about one of your beastly jobs."

As a put-down her frosty statement was a total failure. A look of delighted disbelief spread across his handsome features. Louis Alexander dropped his pen on the desk with a crack, and it rattled noisily across the wood to fall with a clatter on the floor. "You speak Greek?" he reiterated happily.

At that moment the door opened and a pleasant-faced man with fair hair and gray eyes looked in. "Sorry," he apologized. "I didn't realize you'd started interviewing. There's another one here. I'll take her."

"Take them all," Louis Alexander replied expansively, settling back into his swivel armchair. "Miss Hampton"—he frowned as though he had only just taken in her denial of the name—"or—er—well, speaks Greek. I'll leave the rest to you, David. We're going out to lunch."

"We are not going—" Rosalie said furiously.

"Greek?" ejaculated the man called David, his face now suffused in delighted smiles. Then as Alexander signed to him to leave he snapped the door shut, but not before Rosalie saw him make a swift two-fingered victory sign.

Feeling scared, feeling somehow trapped, she smoothed down her dress and said as coolly as she could manage, "Didn't you hear me? I am not Miss Hampton."

"Then who are you?" His eyes raked her, glimmering.

"It's none of your business who I am. And I don't want your job. Goodbye, Mr. Alexander." She spun on her heel and walked with stately dignity toward the door.

But he was too quick for her. Like a leopard, as she had thought the night before, seeing him move swiftly through the gathering dusk of the churchyard, he was at her side, his fingers gripping her wrist. Expertly, with the iron strength of him in his right arm, he swung her around to face him. Then those extraordinary eyes flicked down the length of her body from the top of her silky head to the toes of her slim sandals. "It really doesn't matter who you are, nymph," he said softly. "You're here. And you've applied for the job. Just because my secretary was too involved to announce—"

"I did not apply for the job," she retorted furiously. "The very idea of working for you is quite repugnant to me. How dare you hold me like this? Let me go at once. I'm surprised you get anyone to work for you if you treat them this way."

Ignoring her fury, he looked deeply and disconcertingly into her eyes. "Who are you?" he asked again. "*Haven't* we met somewhere before?"

She and Fay were not alike. How could they be, when they were not blood relations? But people had sometimes commented that they could not distinguish the two girls' voices over the telephone. And had he not seen her, though distantly, under the shadowy trees in the churchyard last night? "No," she replied shakily. "No, we haven't met." How could she broach the subject now? He had relaxed his hold on her wrist. She looked down at it, at the red weals where his fingers had held her in that grip of steel. "Your business methods, if I may say so, are a little tough for me." And his behavior in his private life, she reminded herself, left much to be desired. "I'll go, if you don't mind."

"No," he replied. "No, I can't let you go like this." Now he took her by the arm and with surprising gentleness led her to a chair. "There has clearly been some ridiculous mistake. Let's talk this over." He pressed a small lever and spoke to his secretary through the intercom. "Sylvia, bring two coffees in, please." Then, turning to Rosalie: "Cigarette? No? Do you mind if I do?" he asked with the utmost courtesy.

She shook her head, feeling helpless before this extraordinary man. "Now tell me," he said kindly, "what are you doing here in my office if you don't want a job?"

Tell him. Say he treated Fay abominably. That he was surely responsible, in the long run, for her desperate unhappiness and early demise. Psychosomatic, the doctor had said. Rosalie believed that was another name for a broken heart.

He lit the cigarette, stared at the smoke as it spiraled up toward the ceiling. When she could not bring herself to voice the accusation, he said softly, winningly, "We seem to have got off on the wrong foot, but that can be put right. Have you got a job?"

"Er . . ."

He was onto the truth in a flash. He was quick-witted, all right. "That means no. Now, I have a proposition to make to you, Miss—not Hampton, you say?" She stared at him with frightened eyes, feeling halfway lost already. Had he known the name of his lover's stepsister, who was working abroad? She tried again to voice the accusation, but the words would not come. There was no way she could win with this man, she knew. He would have her out of the office and on the street in the flash of an eye if he wished.

At last she managed, "It doesn't really matter about my name, since I don't intend to work for you."

"Ah, but you are in my office, let us say under false pretenses," he said with a winning smile, "and about to accept my hospitality. Let's be friends, shall we? Job or no job, I mean, let's be friends."

Inexplicably, Rosalie suddenly wanted to laugh. The first bubbles of mirth had risen somewhere inside her. Before she could quell them the door opened and the secretary came in smiling. "Thank you, my dear," said Alexander, warmly courteous. Then he added cunningly, "You didn't get the lady's name, Sylvia. That was very remiss of you."

Innocently, the girl turned to Rosalie. "Yes, it was a bad moment when you came in," she said with a smile. Then, turning to Alexander: "I had two phone calls going and a ring from you." Returning her eyes to Rosalie's face, she went on in a friendly voice. "I didn't get to marking you off the sheet. I know you're not Miss Hampton because she is being interviewed by Mr. Radcliff now."

She could not, without appearing boorish, Rosalie realized, refuse to answer. "Darrien," she said defiantly. "Rosalie Darrien." And then her heart quailed and, compulsively, her eyes were drawn back to those of the man who stood looking watchfully down at her.

"Darrien." He turned the name elegantly over on his tongue. His gaze bored into hers, into her very soul, and uncertainty grew in his eyes. "I could have sworn I'd met you before." Rosalie suppressed a quick sigh of relief. Then he shook his head. "I don't know that name. And yet . . . I have this very certain feeling . . ."

She spoke swiftly to deflect his thoughts. "What is this job you're offering?"

"Can you cook?"

"Of course. But—"

"Then you've got the job. And because you speak Greek, I'll double the pay advertised."

"What job?" This was ridiculous. Warmed by his unexpected courtesy and generosity, Rosalie began to laugh.

23

"You're to take charge of a villa complex we've bought on Mykonos. There will be holiday groups coming every fortnight. You're to meet them . . ."

Mykonos! One of the most beautiful islands in the Aegean. And she had been going back to Greece to look for another job.

Suddenly Rosalie knew why she was here today. There was a price to pay for throwing away a love, a precious life, and she was going to exact that toll. She had not admitted it to herself before, but all at once the anger, the heartbreak, reared up and threatened to consume her. She would pay back this merciless man who thought the world was his oyster, a pretty girl a mere toy to be played with, then tossed aside. She would pay him back somehow, if it was the last thing she did.

"I'll take your job," she said cryptically. "When do I start?"

Chapter Two

It was strange, Rosalie acknowledged to herself as the Boeing 747 roared through the clear sky, traveling side by side with the enemy, the smooth silky texture of his sleeve caressing her bare arm as he moved, the man-smell of him assailing her nostrils. He leaned across her to look through the window at Swiss mountains that even in June lay covered in brilliant white snow; at the Adriatic nudging up through the pretty little Yugoslav islands; at the rough hills of northern Greece.

"Familiar territory?" Louis Alexander looked at her quizzically.

"Not quite. I've been on the island of Corfu, and on Kos. I've never been in the north. It's pretty rugged, I believe. From the hotel where I worked on the eastern side of Corfu we could see the lights of Albania at night, but I understand"—she dimpled wryly—"it's not picnic country. Anyway, no one offered to take me there."

He grinned. "The Communists are relaxing a bit now. I understand you can actually drive through Albania—if you want to, that is. I drove all the way to Greece—not through Albania, I may say—when I first came to negotiate about the villas. I spent nearly a week coming. It was quite a trip," Louis Alexander said nostalgically. He sat back in the seat, looking at her with those discerning eyes, his mouth turning up provocatively at the corners. "Perhaps you and I should have traveled by car. We might have got to know each other on the way."

Rosalie, flushing, turned her head, pretending enormous interest in the panorama of sea and mountains below. She knew he was referring to the fact that she had been stiff with him, but she had no intention of becoming friendly—yet. She had made up her mind to get the measure of the man before planning her campaign. The problem was, he was devastatingly attractive. She was going to have to be careful.

They landed at Athens airport in a haze of June heat. London had been warm, but here the temperature was high in the eighties. As they crossed the tarmac en route to the terminal Rosalie stretched luxuriously, holding her face up to the burning rays of the sun. It was wonderful to be back in Greece again. The atmosphere of the country penetrated even the arrivals area of the warm, hurrying, scurrying airport. Small, dark-skinned, black-haired men shouted excitedly to each other in the Greek way. It was said, Rosalie remembered, holding back a smile, that two Greeks constituted an argument, three a revolution.

"Now," said Louis Alexander after they had collected their bags from the conveyor belt and gone through customs, "if you'll wait here watching the luggage, I'll go and find out what time the plane leaves for Mykonos. Unless"—he glanced at her appraisingly, those tawny eyes glittering with a predatory look— "you'd like to stay the night in Athens and get the ferry in the morning."

"No, thanks." The refusal came automatically. Yet even as Rosalie spoke, her thoughts were dwelling longingly on the possibilities being offered, for she loved the city as she loved the islands.

"We could see the *son et lumière* at the Acropolis," suggested Alexander, his voice soft and winning. "And it would mean a full day on the boat tomorrow. Could be interesting." He waited for her reply, knuckles resting on one lean hip. "The city of Pericles," he said softly, watching her, the warmth of his personality reaching out to engulf her.

She fought back her longing and managed to say stiffly, "This is business, Mr. Alexander. Don't you think we should get on with it?"

He moved a little closer, looking down from his superior height into her upturned face. Deliberately she turned away. "Don't you think the business would be rather more pleasant if you called me Louis, and I called you by your Christian name?"

"Please call me Rosalie," she replied stiffly, "but I'd prefer to call you Mr. Alexander, for the moment anyway."

"Moments are short," he said pointedly, smiling, and then he was moving away from her with long strides, his broad back very straight, head high. She stood looking after him uncertainly, her upper lip caught between her teeth. He was away a long time, twenty minutes or more. She watched him cross the floor on his return, a head taller than the Greeks,

27

elegant, casual. Heavens, but he was handsome! And all man. She could so well understand Fay's falling for him. She thrust the unacceptable memory away.

"We've just missed the plane," he said lightheartedly, and then, in a tone that smacked more of congratulation than commiseration, added, "Bad luck."

Rosalie looked at him sharply. "When does the next plane go?"

"That's the last for today," he replied cheerfully, totally master of the situation as he picked up her bag in one hand and his own in the other. "Let's get a taxi."

She followed him, feeling disturbed. She knew that the desk where he would have made inquiries about the Mykonos plane could not have been too far away. What had he been doing for twenty minutes? She bit back a gnawing suspicion that he had waited for the plane to leave. But what could she do? She wished she were brave enough to ask him to wait while she made her own inquiries. Why should the last plane of the day go at three-thirty? But he was the boss and clearly one who bent the rules to please himself. She followed him out of the airport and settled reluctantly into the back seat of a taxi at his side. They hurtled into Athens in typical Athenian fashion, the driver holding one hand on the horn, pedestrians scattering.

"You'll be used to the wild driving," Louis Alexander said, clearly enjoying himself as they dived in and out of slower cars, missing them by a hairsbreadth. They raced into Syntagma Square, then pulled up precipitately before a large hotel.

"The King George?" Rosalie gave him a mildly querying look as she emerged. "You certainly fly high."

He replied lightly, "Never take second rate when

first rate will do." And taking her arm, he led her up the steps.

Rosalie had never stayed in a deluxe hotel before. She looked around the vast and impressive foyer with its massed flowers, its marble pillars, and felt a quickening of her senses. Alexander certainly had everything it took to attract a girl. Looks. Charm. And now money, it seemed. A night at the King George would cost a pretty penny, she thought, awestruck in spite of every effort toward sangfroid. Then she swung around as a voice said courteously, "Good afternoon, Mr. Alexander. Welcome back." A debonair Greek was shaking Louis Alexander's hand with warmth and genuine pleasure. "We have your suite ready," he said.

"Thank you." Rosalie's head came up, the soft blond hair falling back. She stared at her employer with wide, accusing eyes. "It's always ready," he said smoothly in answer to her unspoken question, but he said it with his head turned so that the manager, if indeed it was he, would not hear. A porter had already picked up the cases and was hurrying toward the elevator.

As Louis Alexander took her arm and prepared to follow she said sharply, "I haven't got my key. The key to my room."

"The bellboy has it," he replied offhandedly.

"Oh." But as she stepped into the lift she saw that the porter had only one key in his hand. She bit back the sharp protest that rose immediately to her lips. She had better not make a scene here. But she was seething as they stepped out into a thickly carpeted passage. "If you think—" she began between clenched teeth, but Louis Alexander cut in, speaking loudly and casually.

"You'll like the suite. It's been in the family, so to

speak, for most of my life. My parents always stayed here when they came to Athens, as they did often to escape the English winter. My father would have had a heart attack if he had found his suite occupied. I don't keep it on, but if it's free— Thank you," he said, pressing some notes into the porter's hand as the man put the luggage down in the foyer and prepared to leave.

Without even pausing to look around, Rosalie pushed the door shut violently with her foot. She backed up against it. "If you think I'm going to share your suite, you had better think again, Mr. Alexander," she stated furiously.

He seemed only mildly surprised. "Why not? It's only the sitting room we share. There are two bedrooms. What's the difference between that and having two rooms adjacent in the passage?"

"It is different. Of course it's different. We're shut off here behind one main door—together." She hurled the denial at him, all her pent-up fury behind it.

"And you think no one will hear you scream?" he asked sarcastically, his well-cut lips curling. "You flatter yourself, Miss Darrien. I'm not in the habit of raping my staff. You can, of course," he added bitingly, "go off alone and find yourself a room somewhere else if you prefer it. I felt, mistakenly no doubt, that this was a good opportunity, since we're going to be working together, to get to know each other. I've brought the plans of the complex with me and hoped to go over them with you this afternoon. You haven't exactly been forthcoming so far. If I'm to leave you in charge of the development I'd quite like to know what sort of person you are." He put both hands on his lean hips and looked down at her, his face hard. "Or would you prefer that I take out one of my friends? I assure you I have many here in Athens. No doubt you could entertain yourself until eight-thirty tomorrow when the boat leaves."

"I'm sorry," Rosalie murmured, putting a hand to her forehead and avoiding the cool stare from those exceptional eyes. She felt suddenly ashamed. "I'm sorry. I didn't mean to blow up like that." Yet she knew why she had. She did not trust this man. Now, facing up to the apparently decent, commonsense side of him, she was confused. "Of course I'd be only too happy to work this evening," she said.

"Good," he approved briskly. His momentary anger disappeared behind a businesslike exterior. He swung around to stride into the sitting room. It was not a big room, but it was spacious, with an air of Edwardian dignity. There was a high stucco ceiling, a large antique desk, and a table and chairs that would seat six. The armchairs were capacious and pretty. It was a place where work could be done in comfort, or, equally, where one might entertain.

"Take your choice," Louis Alexander said courteously, opening the doors leading off the sitting room. The bedrooms were attractive, even luxurious. Rosalie chose the smaller and he carried her bag in, depositing it on the folding trestle. "Tea?"

"Lovely."

He picked up the telephone beside her bed and rang through to the desk. "Now," he said as he replaced the receiver, "you won't need to unpack for a single night, so let's take a quick shower, change, then get down to work. That is, if you want a shower and change of clothes, which I certainly do." He touched the thin material of his shirt, which clung damply to his chest. "Once the air conditioning dries

31

one off it's time to start again. I've been sweating this past hour."

"Me too."

"Oh, no," he reproved. "Even I exaggerate. Horses sweat, men perspire, and ladies gently glow."

She laughed, touched, even faintly disturbed, by his old-world gallantry. "I've been glowing."

He was so easy in his manner when he wanted to be, Rosalie thought, puzzled, as she peeled off her clothes and stepped under the refreshing spray in the gold-and-green bathroom. But he was such an enigma. Five minutes later she was dressed in cool white trousers and a peasant blouse, her damp blond hair secured on the crown of her head with a rubber band. Looking at herself in the mirror, at the young face with the huge, apprehensive eyes, she had an uneasy moment when she wondered if she would be expected to dress in a businesslike manner. This blouse was very feminine and rather low-cut. It was intensely feminine, she admitted, feeling uncertain and disturbed, watching as she turned from the mirror the way it drifted across her arms and swung loosely around her hips. But the air was hot outside. They were bound to go out to eat, she thought, justifying her choice. Scarlet Hungarian embroidery on muslin. She was aware of her sexuality as she never remembered being aware before. But would her new employer want her dressed in prim navy blue? she asked herself.

Nonetheless, she emerged from her room more than a little self-conscious. He was seated at the table with a sheaf of papers spread out before him. He did not even look up. With a sense of anticlimax she crossed the room. He had changed into trousers so well fitting they clung like a second skin, and he wore a beautifully cut silk shirt of a pale bronze color, open to the waist so that the mat of fine hair on his chest lay bare. Momentarily Rosalie caught her breath at the man's sheer male beauty, and then there was a discreet knock at the door and a waiter entered with a tray of tea and honey cakes.

"Thank you," Louis Alexander said briefly, without lifting his eyes from the paper. "Put it on the table." With just the right touch of discretion he managed, still without looking up, to slip some notes into the waiter's hand as he left. "Milk and sugar, Rosalie," he said in a detached voice. "Two spoons. Now, here's a map of the island, when you're ready." He was smoothing an enormous sheet of paper across the table. "We haven't been allowed to build anything yet. Maybe we won't have to. I've bought three villas, all quite close together. At least, my partner bought them. His name's Spiro."

"Oh, you have a Greek partner?" She was surprised.

"Never make life difficult for yourself when you can make it easy," Louis Alexander murmured lazily. "Spiro has his faults—he's idle, charming, and girl-mad. You'll have to watch yourself with him," he said casually, just as though he himself were the most trustworthy man in the world, Rosalie thought wryly. "But it's not easy to go into business here without a Greek partner. They know the ropes, which an Englishman does not. Spiro is a sleeping partner, by the way. He has his own little hotel—or rooming house, to be more precise. And a restaurant, which we may be using. That's open to negotiation. He's only going to be available to you as a consultant. If we don't know how to go about something, we ask Spiro. If we run up against officialdom, we put Spiro onto it. The villas are fairly primitive, but that's what people seem to want on this kind of holiday. There's going to be windsurfing a little later. I haven't got the gear out there yet. And sailing, of course. I'm trying to buy my own caïque, but I haven't succeeded yet. The Greeks, it seems, are proud of their boats and don't like relinquishing them. Can you sail?"

She had poured the tea and was carrying his cup across the room to him. In her other hand was a plate on which she had put one of the honey cakes. "Yes," she replied. She had done some sailing last summer on the island of Corfu.

"Good. All we need is our own caïque." He looked up, grinning, and did a double take. "Well," he said, sitting back in his chair, looking her up and down admiringly so that she found herself blushing with embarrassment. "So I hired a Middle European hand-embroidered peasant for an assistant! You might have warned me." He went on gazing at her as though he had never seen her before, and as he gazed she thought there was a softening of those hard features and a predatory look growing in his eyes.

"I bought it in London. In—er—the Portobello Road market—very cheaply," Rosalie said defensively. "It's the coolest thing I have."

He took the tea, his eyes alight, his mouth sardonically amused. "I see you're a girl who can capitulate in style," he said admiringly, increasing her apprehension. What did he mean? And then, as she racked her brain for a reply, he said in a more businesslike tone, "Now, down to work." He wolfed down the honey cake without appearing to notice it.

They sipped their tea while he explained about the terraces that were being constructed to provide the houses he had bought with vine-enclosed outdoor relaxation areas. Briefly he outlined his proposed catering arrangements, went into detail on his advertising campaign. Rosalie shifted the teacups over to a side table. As she moved he leaned back in his chair, crossed his legs, and watched her with disconcerting attentiveness. "Cigarette?" he asked as she returned, flipping a packet out of the breast pocket in his elegant shirt.

"No, thanks." He lit his own, somehow managing to infuse the mundane act with élan.

"Before the first guests arrive you're going to have a certain amount of negotiation with the locals," he told her. "That's why it was essential that I should find someone who speaks Greek. Food is so reasonable, as you know, that I'm hoping to get a good arrangement going with Spiro's restaurant to feed the guests. That way I avoid importing English cooks and the guests can have the genuine food of the country. But here's the catch." He gave her that cool, appraising look she was beginning to know. "Greek food, as you know, is rather repetitive. There are only about five recipes and, tasty though they are, English tourists can get very tired of them. They can get tired of the eternal cucumber-and-tomato salad too," he added on a light laugh, "but they'll have to put up with that, as it's too difficult to get anything else. I'm going to ask you to be prepared, if you get some insular and finicky guests—and you will—to concoct some English-type meals, say every three or four days." He sounded considerate, almost gentle. Then, showing his bleak side, he added, "I always say people who're not adventurous with their food ought to stay at home, but when in business one must be businesslike. It is a fact there are a lot of unadventurous people around, and first and foremost I'm in this for the money. By the way, how's the teapot? Are those rotten little tea bags good for another cup? Why foreigners can't make tea properly I don't know," he grumbled. "Somebody ought to tell them it's the sweepings from the tea factory that go into bags."

Laughing, Rosalie went across the room to refill his cup.

"I realize I've only given you a brief sketch of what's going on," Louis Alexander said apologetically, leaning back in his chair and stretching his long arms, looking her up and down again appreciatively from head to toe as she filled his cup. "But there wasn't time. I had a lot of loose ends to tie up in order to get away by the arranged date. Have you tasted the honey cakes? They're not bad, although they won't do that luscious figure of yours any good. Bring me another, will you, and then we'll settle down to talk finance."

It was nearly six o'clock when they folded up the papers. "Well," said Louis Alexander, "are you quite happy?"

She answered dryly but straightforwardly. "It's quite an assignment. I see now why you waited until you got me here before laying it all before me."

He glowered. "You're saying you've been tricked?"

"No." She wanted to say she thought him wily, for want of a better word, but she did not dare. These were the details she had asked for in London. He had made excuses, saying, "We'll talk. But for the moment I'm very tied up." She wondered if he really had been so busy, or if in fact this system of getting the cat in the bag before planning the next move was part of a clever business routine. Well, she wasn't going to allow him to take advantage of her. She was not going to easily forget that Fay had been destroyed by her brush with this ruthless man.

36

She said, keeping her voice cool, "I'm not certain now that the pay is adequate for what I'm taking on."

"It's higher than you've earned before, I'll warrant."

She lifted her head and faced him squarely, though there were butterflies in her stomach. "I was working in a taverna before. I wasn't using my brains. There was no planning involved. No responsibility. And I got supplementary tips. There's a great deal of responsibility and decision making in this job as well as sheer hard work. And," she added, playing her trump card with what she hoped was flair, though the butterflies danced madly and she was afraid her apprehension showed, "I am the only girl you found who speaks Greek. That clearly is worth something."

"The pay is negotiable," he growled, capitulating, then added sharply, "But don't forget I expect a good day's work for a good day's pay."

He had a genius for rubbing her the wrong way. "You're asking for a good many good days' work," she retorted sharply. "That's my point."

He stared at her in that disconcerting way he had and then, to her utter astonishment, he named a figure that was half as much again as he had offered in the office in London. Stifling a gasp, she nonetheless managed to say coolly, "That will do very well, Mr. Alexander."

"You have me over a barrel, don't you?"

"No, I don't think so. I agreed to come for a certain amount, not knowing what I was coming to. I felt, this afternoon when I saw the sheer extent of the job, that you may have deliberately kept me in ignorance." She raised her eyes, using everything she had of strength and resistance to meet his, quailing inwardly but determined to say what she felt must be said. It was clear that if she did not stand up for herself this man would ride roughshod over her all the way. His eyes were cold, hard amber now, his jaw square, his mouth cruel. It was all she could do not to react with sheer fright. She wanted to jump up and run.

"Don't ever accuse me of cheating again," he said icily. And then he repeated, "Ever."

There was a shocked moment when the breath seemed to have left Rosalie's body. Had she done that? Had she accused him of cheating? She had not intended to. In the vibrant, tearing silence a rap came at the door. Louis Alexander barked, "Come in," and a waiter appeared carrying a silver tray. "Your tickets for the *son et lumière*," he said politely, crossing the room and deferentially extending the tray.

Louis Alexander took them in silence, dropped a couple of notes on the tray, and, scowling, said, "Thank you."

"That's what I mean," flared Rosalie, losing her wits and going to pieces as soon as the door closed after the waiter. "You bulldoze your way through life, don't you? I'm not a fool, Mr. Alexander. I'm an intelligent girl who expects to be consulted. I don't expect a—a partnership. But there should be a kind of mutual understanding between us. You've only known me five minutes and you've been—been— you've taken me over—you're—you're . . . When did you order those tickets? Not since we came here. You knew, all the time, that we were going to stay in Athens tonight. You booked the suite. I won't stand—"

"You can stand anything for five minutes," Louis Alexander cut in softly, and then he took her hands and raised them to his lips. "I like a girl with spirit," he said, but he said it arrogantly, as though he knew he could break that spirit if and when he chose. As his lips touched her fingers a fire went right through her and, frightened, she jerked her hands away. Fay had had spirit, she remembered. Fay, from whom it seemed he had taken everything, even life itself. She must not forget why she was here. Not for the job. Not for the money. She was here for revenge.

Chapter Three

"There's the Tudor Hall restaurant on the top floor," said Louis Alexander. "It has a magnificent view of the Acropolis. But you'd have to get out of that fetching outfit if we ate there, and what a pity that would be. Shall we just go and have a drink at the Causette Bar, make our way to the *son et lumière*, then eat when the show's over?"

Rosalie nodded. She already felt drained from the several clashes she had had with this man. She was not of a mind to disagree with anything he said. And besides, a drink would relax her.

They went down to the sumptuous bar where guests relaxed elegantly. There were female tourists beautifully coiffured, escorted by debonair men in summer suits; dark Greek ladies bejeweled and elegantly turned out with their black glossy hair smooth as a raven's wing. And there were men like Louis Alexander in subtly designed clothes that looked casual and cost the earth; girls like her in slim-fitting jeans, with perhaps that one deliberately obvious accessory which she did not have, something that whispered of wealth: a diamond bracelet on a suntanned arm emerging from faded denim, a Louis Féraud blouse aglitter with Christian Dior chains. For a moment Rosalie was taken aback. And then she remembered that her secondhand blouse bought economically in the Portobello Road market could have been sold new at a very high price in Knightsbridge. Perhaps that accounted for her employer's surprise when he first saw her in these clothes. He knew good garments when he saw them. She noticed several pairs of eyes on her and knew with a sigh of relief that she was, if only accidentally, holding her own.

They took a taxi through the darkening streets of the city and walked up the winding path to the amphitheater. It was a beautiful evening, the moon already rising in a star-studded velvet sky. Presently the swirling spotlights picked out the different sections of the magnificent ruins, marble white against the sky, and the deep, beautiful, familiar voices of famous actors—Laurence Olivier, John Gielgud—picked up the sad and glorious, brilliant and savage history of Greece. Although she had seen the show several times before, Rosalie was lost again in its beauty. She forgot the man sitting beside her. Forgot everything but the glory of the moment.

She came back to earth with the clapping. "It was wonderful. Wonderful," she murmured as they rose and filed back to the entrance. "Thank you for bringing me." She had forgotten, also, her anger at having been taken over. She looked up and was surprised to see that Alexander's eyes were gentle in his tanned face, and she realized that he, too, had been deeply moved.

They found a cab and climbed in. In his deeply authoritative voice Louis Alexander gave an address. "It's quite a modest restaurant I'm taking you to," he said, "but the food's excellent."

To Rosalie's surprise and delight there were fish tanks flanking the doorway. Lobsters, balanced in their awkward fashion on small rocks, seemed to be looking curiously at her with their beady eyes while fish swam rhythmically up and down.

"Oh, no!" Rosalie gasped, laughing, dismayed. "You're not going to ask me to choose my own dinner, then have the creature murdered for it?"

"While you wait," Alexander assured her lightly. "Are you so softhearted?"

"Yes," she replied queasily. "Yes, I think I am."

"Nobody's asking you to pat a pet lamb, then watch it being skewered into kebab squares," he pointed out reasonably as they were shown to their seats. She sat down, put her hands over her face, and said, "I'll have lobster. But even that ugly brute I refuse to identify. I want an anonymous lobster, if you please."

The waiter and Alexander joined in her wry laughter. "But they are so fresh, madame."

She took her hands away from her face. "Too fresh by half for me," she returned wryly.

"And for starters?" her escort queried. "There are some good mixed salads. Or how about *avgolémono?* That's a chicken broth thickened with rice and eggs and flavored with lemon, in case you don't know." Inexplicably wanting to please him, she nodded. "I'll have that." And then she told herself sternly that this unaccustomed luxury, combined with the man's confident and smooth manner, was having just the effect he wanted. She sat up straight, forcing herself to feel brisk, critical. There was nothing modest about this place, she told herself, looking around at the well-heeled diners, and a quick glance at the menu confirmed her judgment. Louis Alexander certainly did himself well.

He ordered an apéritif. "Ouzo? Or have you tried *mastíka?* It's sweeter and more scented." Rosalie had tried it, and liked it. It came flanked by an elaborate plate of canapés spread with *brik,* a red caviar, and *taramosaláta,* that delicious preparation of fish roes. They drank retsina, a rugged white wine flavored with resin, an inheritance from the ancients. Louis Alexander had always liked its peculiar flavor, he said, and Rosalie had grown accustomed to it during her stay in the Greek islands.

"I hope you've got all the tourist spiel at your fingertips," he said. "You're going to have to be a fount of knowledge as well as cook, hostess, wine steward, skivvy, nurse, mother confessor . . ."

She laughed weakly. The wine was already going to her head. "And don't ask for an extra fee," he added, with a mock growl.

"I believe originally retsina came across from Crete in oak barrels, isn't that right? But they ran out of oak and had to make the barrels of pine. The resin from the wood flavored it so that later on when they had to make the barrels of oak again the Greeks missed the taste and took to adding resin. Isn't that so?"

"Top marks." They looked at each other and smiled. "There's another story that the Greeks were drinking too much wine so the authorities added resin to it so as to make it less palatable. But they accustomed themselves to the taste and won't have it without, now. You could tell half the guests one story

43

and the other half the second story, then sit back and amuse yourself listening to the ensuing arguments." They laughed merrily together.

I'm being weak. Foolish. I'm playing with fire, Rosalie thought suddenly. She looked down at the glass of wine, and all at once she did not care. It had been such a surprising day. Such a long day, since six o'clock when she had wakened at her grandmother's house, to ten-thirty Greek time which, come to think of it, was only eight-thirty English time. It has not been such a long day, she admitted to herself. Just overwhelming. I'll get my defenses back in place tomorrow, she thought, feeling soft and vulnerable. Feeling good. Tomorrow will be the start of the road to revenge. Tomorrow.

And yet it did not happen like that, after all. They walked back to Syntagma Square through the narrow streets, still busy at midnight because the Greeks are night people. Those shouting, arguing groups of men were on every corner, just as though they had not dispersed since Rosalie was here last summer. The wine had warmed her, the food pleased her, and Louis Alexander was at his most charming. They went up in the lift together and walked silently along the luxuriously carpeted hallway side by side. Louis Alexander put his key in the door.

Suddenly, overwhelmingly, Rosalie was aware, as she had been earlier in the day before her employer convinced her with his smooth talking, that they were indeed alone behind a locked door. A man and a woman, young, attracted to each other in spite of themselves, vulnerable to human passions, human weaknesses. She caught her breath as the door swung to behind her and in her panic to get past him and into her room she caught her foot against his and stumbled. His arms shot out and closed around her. She felt the iron strength of them, the warmth too. Her senses reeled. Suddenly he had swung her upright, her small breasts pressed against his broad chest, the man-smell of him assailing her nostrils.

"Let me go," she gasped in a panic, more afraid of herself than of him.

"I'll let you go," he said softly, "when I've finished with you. You're vulnerable, aren't you? By heaven, you're vulnerable. You're the most feminine little thing I've met in many a long day. And I have met you before, haven't I?" He took her small chin between hard fingers and jerked her face up to his, looking into her eyes. "I know your voice and sometimes I think I know you. There are things you say I've heard before—or it's in the way you say them. But I just can't—" He broke off to demand grittily, "What's your game? Who are you?"

Panic-stricken, she tried to jerk away, but he held her as though with bands of steel. "Don't think I've forgotten the way you broke into my office," he said. "Told me you didn't want the job. Then suddenly decided you did. I'm not the fool you take me for, Miss Rosalie Darrien. You came to my office for a reason, didn't you? And now's the moment," he went on softly, insistently, "to tell me all about it."

She fought to extricate herself and failed. He was looking down into her face, his eyes cruel. Then suddenly his head came down, his lips hard against her warm mouth, his tongue seeking hers. She felt herself lifted on a giddy spiral of desire and all the strength seemed to go out of her body so that she relaxed against him, limp and helpless in her fight not to match his passion with her own.

"Let me go," she moaned as soon as he freed her lips, not wanting to go at all, fighting herself as well as him.

"A tiger in lamb's clothing," he marveled. And then suddenly he pushed her from him, put a hand into his pocket, and pulled out a packet of cigarettes. "All right." He slapped the words at her. "Out with it."

There was only one thing to do. She sidestepped, dashed for her room, flung the door wide, slipped through, swung it shut, and reached for the key. But he was too quick for her. The door burst open again as though it had a life of its own, and he was there. The cigarettes were flying, spilling across the carpet. He picked her up like a feather and flung her down on one of the beds with a jolt that shook the very breath out of her.

"Don't look at me like that," he said, retrieving his cigarettes. "I've never raped anyone, and I'm not going to start it now. I just want you to know who's the boss around here. When a girl dresses up the way you're dressed, looks the way you look, there's a clear indication that she doesn't expect an employer/employee relationship. And if you don't expect it, whether subconsciously or consciously, you won't get it. I'm all man, in case you hadn't noticed," he sneered, "and no girl, however beautiful and efficient and apparently indispensable, plays ducks and drakes with me. Now, are you going to tell me what you're up to, or not?"

Shaken, torn, beside herself with fury, Rosalie pulled herself into a sitting position. She did not dare put her feet on the floor. She said, "All right, you're all man. But you've got the imagination of a woman. And you're the most conceited, arrogant, insufferable—" She stopped because he was advancing toward her, his stride slow and measured, a cigarette between his lips, the lighted match in one hand. He kept coming until he was right beside the bed. Then he leaned down, so close that she felt his hot breath on her cheek. When he spoke his voice was low, disturbing.

"Yes," he said softly, "but you like 'em that way, don't you!" Then, before she could get her breath, he had swung on his heel, crossed the room, and banged the door behind him.

Rosalie lay awake hour after hour far into the morning, her troubled thoughts running backward and forward in her mind. Little had she realized when she set out so confidently to avenge Fay's death the complications that lay in wait for her. Little had she realized when she saw Louis Alexander in his office how powerless, how essentially feminine, how vulnerable she would find herself when locked in combat with this man. "Frailty, thy name is woman," Shakespeare had said. How right he was, she realized now. Well, she would just have to toughen up, because she was going to win this battle and no mistake. "I'll pay you back, Louis Alexander," she said to herself as she at last drifted off to sleep, "if it's the last thing I do."

Next morning she was awakened by a brisk knock at the door. "Coffee, croissants, and Greek cake," said that now familiar firm voice, but with a laugh in it. "Do you want it in bed on a tray?"

"I'll be up in two shakes," Rosalie called breathlessly, scrambling out of bed still only half awake. Conscious of her nakedness, she reached blindly for her clothes, apprehensive that this man at whose mercy she found herself, this man who clearly considered the world his oyster, should burst through the door. She rushed headlong into the bathroom and turned on the cold shower, which was very far from cold. Wrapping a vast fluffy towel around her slimly curved figure, she hurtled back into the bedroom, flung herself into a bikini, stepped into slim-fitting

47

jeans, and pulled on a yellow cotton shirt. It took only a moment to flip her blond hair into order and touch a lipstick to her mouth.

His bag was by the door ready to go and he was standing at the table, courteously if impatiently waiting for her. He looked debonair and handsome in a casual blue shirt and jeans that hugged his hips, emphasizing his overwhelming virility. With an amused expression he drew out her chair, then took his own. "Quite the domestic scene," he commented as he passed the croissants. "I didn't order Nescafé. I assume you've acquired a taste for this devilish Turkish stuff."

She smiled. "It's great. The first time I tasted it the cup seemed so small I upended it and drank the lot at once."

"And got a mouthful of grounds. I can imagine." Louis Alexander chuckled. "And how about the cake? Have you absorbed the Greek way of life sufficiently to enjoy cake for breakfast?"

She shook her head. "I've never managed to cope with that. How much time have we got?"

He glanced at his watch. "It's seven-thirty. The boat leaves in an hour. I've paid the bill. We've only to step into the taxi. The doorman will have it at the door at eight. I've got the tickets."

He meant the hotel had got his tickets, just as they were arranging to have his taxi waiting, Rosalie thought, reluctantly impressed at the way this man seemed to have the whole world watching out for his comfort. They ate their breakfast comparatively quickly. Rosalie locked her suitcase; then Louis Alexander rang for a porter. In no time at all they were scurrying through the early-morning traffic on the way to the port of Piraeus. The big ferryboat was waiting at the wharf, porters, ticket collectors, officials shouting noisily to and at each other, gesticulating in the typical Greek way. They went aboard and Alexander led her directly to the sun deck. Already the early-morning sun was hot, blazing out of a cornflower-blue sky. "Mind if I strip?" asked Rosalie, feeling light-hearted and happy at the thought of a full day in the sun.

"Strip?" Alexander queried lazily, watching her with eyes half closed as she peeled off her blouse and jeans. "That top looks like surplus gear to me."

She flushed. "I haven't gone topless yet," she said modestly. And in the circumstances, I'm not likely to, she thought. That would be asking for trouble. "June," she murmured, shutting her eyes and turning her face to the sun. "I wonder if there will be any wild flowers left over from spring."

"I doubt it. But you'll have two months before the *meltémi* blows up."

"That's the beastly hot wind that comes in August? Yes. I can do without that."

There was a blast from the ship's siren. People were scurrying up the companionway, looking for seats in the shade or the sun according to their inclinations. Some young people settled down on the deck, leaning against their packs. Alexander gave her a sideways look and said humorously, "I don't want to tempt you to ask for another raise, but have you got a spiel ready on the Greek legends? You do know some mythology, I presume."

She looked at him coldly but managed to keep her voice light. "So I'm to be campfire entertainer too? You strike a hard bargain, Mr. Alexander."

He put a hand on her bare forearm. In spite of herself a tremor ran from fingers to shoulder. "Please," he entreated. "We're surely old friends now. I've carried you across the threshold of your bedroom. We've shared an intimate breakfast. What more is necessary before you'll call me Louis? I know in Victorian times a woman would actually call her husband Mr., but this is the late twentieth century."

"Louis." She said it at last, thinking of Fay, and his name had the bitterness of gall in her mouth. But she must play her part. "Oh, well. Yes, I do know something of the Greek legends, Louis. I also know that Mykonos has no history. You should have chosen the island of Delos, next door. The Sacred Isle. I believe it was one of the most important civilizations, even B.C. One of the five trading ports on the run between Turkey and Amalfi in Italy; the most important one."

"That's right. But Delos is given over to archaeologists. You can go over for day visits, but you can't stay there. I believe there is some sort of hostel for the archaeological setup. And a small hotel. Maybe for stranded tourists, or keen ancient-history students. I'll take you there on your day off," he added.

She said wryly, "So I'm to have a day off!"

"All work and no play makes Jack a dull boy. And I can't bear dull people. Sure you're to have a day off—sometime. Did you know Artemis and Apollo were born on Delos?"

"While Leto, the mortal mother, clutched the branches of a palm tree. It sounded like a difficult birth." She found herself laughing with him, almost companionably. "Fill me in on that pagan legend, Louis. If I knew it, I've forgotten." Surprisingly, after all, the name slid lightly over her tongue.

"Leto was pregnant by the randy god Zeus. Hera, Zeus' wife, sent the serpent Python to persecute her. She ran and ran, but no country would give her sanctuary. They wouldn't risk Hera's anger."

"I don't blame them. There is no fury like that of a woman scorned, it's said."

"So Zeus, in desperation for her safety, fixed the floating island Delos to the ocean floor with a diamond pin."

"That's right. Now I remember. There's another version that says Poseidon made Delos rise out of the sea. There's a mountain on Delos, Mount Cynthus?"

"Yes. Zeus crouched on top of it guarding his lover during the birth. It's quite a place. You could take your guests there on your day off."

"I thought there was going to be a catch to that day off," Rosalie murmured darkly. "Isn't this sun marvelous?" She leaned back in her seat, gazing blissfully out across the water. They slid past Cape Sounion. The ruins of the temple of Poseidon rose starkly against the sky. After that it was all islands. The ferryboat slid in and out among them, stopping only twice to disgorge passengers. They came in to Mykonos in late afternoon as the sun began to sink.

It was a white island, jammed with little square boxes of houses one upon the other up the rocky slope that faced the harbor. "Oh, isn't it lovely!" Rosalie clapped her hands delightedly. "I'm going to adore this." She swung around in her excitement. Louis was watching her through sleepy, heavy-lidded eyes, an enigmatic smile on his face. His long legs in their fitted jeans were stretched out before him, his brown torso gleaming where little drops of sweat stood out on shoulders and chest.

"Glad to have a satisfied customer," he replied affably.

A fleet of launches came out to meet them. Short, burly, black-haired men with strident voices bundled the luggage aboard and hurried the passengers after

51

it. The little boats rocked frenziedly on the choppy water. "It always blows in the afternoon," Louis had said. They sped to shore in a shower of spray and disembarked into a crowd of short, dark-haired men shouting lively greetings. Elderly, sallow-faced women in widow's weeds stood by, smiling a welcome. A young Greek elbowed his way through the crowd shouting "Louis!" and pumped Louis' hand delightedly. "An: You made it! I met the plane."

"We missed it," lied Louis with a charming smile at Rosalie. "Spiro, allow me to present my assistant, shortly to become our manager, Miss Rosalie Darrien." Spiro was young, lively, slim-hipped and black-eyed with the longest, sootiest lashes Rosalie had ever seen on a man. His smile was a flash of gleaming white teeth. "Spiro is my partner," Louis explained unnecessarily.

The Greek looked Rosalie up and down from the top of her blond head to her sandaled feet with frank admiration. "Very pleased to meet you," he declared and slapped Louis boisterously on the back. "Come. I take your bags. Is no point in taxi. Not far."

"And don't try any tricks in front of Miss Darrien," growled Louis. "Behind that pretty face there's a brain. She speaks Greek."

"Spiks Greek!" echoed Spiro, marveling. "That is good." He tossed her another admiring look, then picked up the bags and set off along the waterfront where the cobblestones were quaintly ringed with white paint and where tavernas with bright awnings emitted the aroma of coffee; where dark-eyed men with black hairy arms sat playing cards at small tables and the air was vibrant with chatter and argument. They passed holidaymakers lounging in their bright, brief clothes at small tables, sipping drinks and watching the activity on the quay with mild curiosity. A pink pelican wandered among the fishing caïques on the beach looking for tidbits. Spiro led them away from the quay into the narrow streets of the town.

"The shops are typical tourist traps," Louis told Rosalie, indicating with a hand gesture one that was spilling over with embroidered blouses, heavy knit jumpers, shawls, and tiny windmills, "but they have some attractive stuff for the discerning buyer." They followed Spiro's hurrying steps through the idling crowds and emerged shortly on a narrow dusty road that led up a steep slope with a pretty windmill at the top. Spiro was waiting for them. "There's our complex," said Louis, pointing. "Those three villas set up there in front of the windmill. It's a great position."

"You will be surprised, Miss Darrien," said Spiro ingenuously, "for there is not much there." Rosalie shot Louis a querying look, but his head was turned away. A dart of suspicion shot through her. They slowed, inevitably, on the hill, for though it was nearly five o'clock heat lay heavily around them.

The three villas were typical of the island's architecture, square, white-painted, with sloping roofs covered in apricot-colored tiles. Five mangy, half-starved cats formed a pathetic welcoming committee. Spiro shooed them away. Rosalie looked at them with compassion. She knew all about Greece's cats. They were everywhere, in the streets, hanging around restaurants, on the quays looking for fish. There was no way anyone could feed them all.

They came up on a wide tiled terrace and Rosalie stood looking around with delight. The air here was crystal clear. Sparkling. In front, across the rooftops of the town, was the harbor, and to the left, the big bay. Islands lay dotted in the distance. That delightful storybook windmill, stark white with bat-wing sails and deep-set oblong windows that she had seen from the bottom of the hill, was above them.

She said, "Oh, it's lovely! How I am going to enjoy this!"

Then she felt a hand on her shoulder and Louis said, "No job's worth a candle if you don't enjoy it." She swung around warmly to meet his enigmatic eyes.

"I shall. I certainly shall."

There was a great curtain of blazing bougainvillea shading the end of the terrace from the setting sun, and a grapevine trailed across a frame which would shelter three quarters of it from the burning midday heat. Beneath the vine stood a long table and some folding chairs.

"But please to look inside," Spiro said warningly, dumping the bags down and producing a key. He unlocked the front door. Here was a wide tiled hall and leading off it half a dozen doors. Spiro led the way. "Bedroom. Empty yet, you see." Another bedroom. Empty. "Furniture coming," offered Spiro with an uncertain look at Louis.

"When?" snapped Louis. Spiro shrugged. "The first batch of guests are due in two weeks," Louis said coldly. "I expected a better reception than this, Spiro."

"One room ready," said Spiro, flinging open another door with confidence. There were two narrow beds, a long mirror, and a small chest of drawers here. Rosalie frowned as she felt apprehension creeping in. She turned and went into the kitchen. It was a big room, but bare. There were one or two pots hanging on the wall. An old-fashioned sink. A modern cooker. With sinking heart she turned to the bathroom. It was beautifully tiled in green and white and there was a shower. Suspiciously, for she knew Greek plumbing could not always be relied upon, she turned on a tap. Nothing. She turned to see Spiro watching her, his expression apologetic.

"Will turn on," he said placatingly.

Pushing her apprehensions regarding the one bedroom into the back of her mind, she went out through the front door. "Since it doesn't rain here in the summer, the terrace is to be the dining room?" She gave Louis a querying look. He nodded. She addressed Spiro. "What about the other two villas? Have they any furniture?" He shook his head. "Not yet."

"Very well," she said in a firm, businesslike voice, "I'd like you to help Louis carry one of those beds into the small room at the back of the villa."

"Sorry," said Spiro, looking uncertainly from one to the other, "are fixed."

"What do you mean, 'fixed'?" she demanded. Sweat was standing out on her forehead, and it was not entirely due to the heat of the day.

"Fixed to floor. Came with purchase, you see." Momentarily, Rosalie was at a loss for words. Then she pulled herself together. This job was going to be no sinecure, and the sooner she got on top of it, with all its potential twists and turns, the better.

Avoiding Louis' eyes, she said bleakly, "Then unless Mr. Alexander wishes to sleep on the dining table I suggest you either have another bed sent up here this evening, or else take him home to your own residence."

"Louis," he corrected blandly with perfect sangfroid, turning his head so that Spiro could not hear. "I thought we'd agreed, after the intimate nature of last night, that it should be Louis and Rosalie."

He was incorrigible. But she was on her mettle now and ready for his wily tricks. She picked up her bag and, holding her head high, carried it into the furnished room. "I'm sure you two men are capable of dealing with this small matter," she said coldly. "I leave it entirely to you." But her heart was pounding and there was very little confidence in her.

Chapter Four

Somehow, miraculously, another bed arrived. It came on a strange contraption that was like a motorized handcart. There were no private cars on the island, Spiro had told Rosalie. Only buses, a few taxis, and one or two little trucks, used mainly by builders.

"Put the bed in one of the other villas," she ordered the removal men, jumping up from the dining table at which she was compiling lists and standing firmly in the doorway to bar their entry. "It isn't to come in here. In fact, put it in the bottom one," she added. Louis was for the moment out of earshot measuring up an area at the back of the lower house where a concrete terrace was to be laid the next day. Apparently things were not so bad as they had at first appeared. Mattresses, bed linen, cutlery, and kitchenware had in fact arrived, but in Louis' absence no one had bothered to get them out of storage. Spiro was indeed a sleeping partner in this venture, Rosalie thought wryly. There was clearly going to be no relying on him.

By eight o'clock they had done as much as was possible for that day. The water in all three villas had been turned on, and the warehouse, which was only a few streets away, notified that everything they had in storage must be delivered the next day at an early hour. "There should be no trouble about that," she told Louis. "If there's one thing Greeks are good at, it's getting up early." Their long after-lunch siesta was acceptable in view of the advantages of a five or six o'clock start in the cool of the day.

Rosalie was rummaging in her bag for a fresh pair of sandals when there was a soft sound behind her. She swung around with a soft gasp. "Oh, it's you!" After the strain of the past day and night her nerves were on edge. "Sorry to snap like that," she murmured. "I guess I'm tired."

"It's time to knock off," Louis replied. "I've had some sheets sent around for your virgin couch." He tossed them onto one of the beds. "Pity. Such a waste of bed linen."

"You've really got a nerve," she flared.

"No one ever got anywhere without a certain degree of nerve," he replied laconically. "How about a meal? I'm starving, and you must be, too. Actually," he added, "what you need is a relaxing drink."

She knew he spoke the truth. She had lain awake too long last night. In spite of the pleasant day, the strain at either end of it had taken its toll. If only he were not such an enigma. If only she did not have to be eternally on her mettle. On her guard, too. If only she could be certain of trusting herself, she thought as she washed in the lukewarm water from the cold tap in the bathroom. That was a hurdle she had not expected to have to surmount—her own sexuality. How she had hated Louis Alexander that day she met him in his London office! But since they had been together, like rock before a pickax, her hate had been chipped away by the sheer strength of his formidable personality.

She went back into her bare little room and took a dress from her suitcase. She shook it out and held it up, eyeing it critically. A very pretty Indian cotton patterned in red and ocher flowers, and it had a cool, loose line. She slipped it over her head and eyed herself in the mirror, her mind a whirlpool of questions about herself. She released the rubber band on the crown of her head, allowing her hair to fall loosely around her shoulders. "Heavens," she muttered to herself, biting her lip. "You're all girl, aren't you, Rosalie Darrien!" Blond hair. Eyes—hadn't her grandmother said when trying to boost her ego that she had pretty violet eyes? She had thought of them always as a peculiar shade of blue. Now, yes, they were violet. And her mouth had softened. Become vulnerable. Rosalie had never seen herself like this before. Ripened, she thought confusedly. Yes, that was it. She tore the dress off, donned an old pair of jeans with a cotton shirt, and turning her back on the mirror began furiously to brush her hair. "If you don't want trouble, don't court it," she said to herself between clenched teeth. Somewhere inside her another voice was saying that there was a side of herself she did not know. Had perhaps never known. "We're working together. It's a working relationship, and don't you forget it. And don't"—she turned and glowered at herself in the mirror—"forget why you're here, and what he did to Fay."

A voice from the window called, "Ready?" Suddenly he was there, his head and shoulders framed by the patch of sky visible through the window. And he was laughing. "I liked the dress," he said. "I've a feeling you like it, too. Why don't you put it back on?"

"How dare you!" she flared. "You—you—you peeping Tom! How dare you spy on me!" She felt exposed, and suddenly close to tears. He said with surprising gentleness, "I was coming down the hill and I saw your reflection in the windowpane. You had a dress on. I'm sorry. I didn't mean to intrude on your privacy. Now I arrive and you've done a quick change into working gear. Won't you dress up for me?" She was looking at him stonily. Suddenly her heart turned over. She had an appalling feeling she was going to cry.

She picked up the flimsy dress from the bed. "I—I was just trying this on to—to—to see if it was terribly crushed. There's no iron here."

"There'll be an iron tomorrow," he said kindly. "I'm going out onto the terrace to wait. I'd always rather take a pretty girl than a working partner to dinner. That's all I meant. Spiro is expecting us in an hour. There's time to sit awhile on the quay and drink a glass of ouzo while we watch the fishing boats go out."

"Okay." She looked down at the dress, her mind cloudy with uncertainty. Of course she must go decently dressed. It was insulting to appear in these old trousers when a man—whoever he was—asked one out to dinner. Penitently, she removed them and put the dress back on. But she did not look in the glass again.

Louis smiled his approval but did not comment as she came out onto the terrace.

They found a vacant table and two chairs on the cobblestones outside one of those little tavernas where the men were playing cards. All around the gaily clad tourists were chattering, drinking coffee, drinking wine. The caïques were abustle with busy fishermen folding golden-colored nylon nets, stowing away their night's provisions, checking their engines. The air was full of the salty tang and sounds of the sea. Louis said, "I'm going to order you an ouzo."

"It's got the kick of a mule," she protested. It was a colorless, harmless-looking spirit and all the Greeks drank it. It was the cheap drink, the local tipple. But Rosalie was very conscious that she had had little to eat all day. "Ouzo on an empty stomach . . ." she demurred.

"Dr. Alexander orders it." Those eyes that were so expressive, by turns so hard, so gentle, were watchful. He knew, she thought, glancing away, that the day, or rather the two days since she had left London, with their shocks and apprehensions, had finally taken their toll. A passing waiter paused and he ordered. "Two ouzos, please." For the first time she heard him speak in Greek.

"Where did you learn the language?"

"Like you, I worked here. In school holidays when my parents came I came too, but a lad doesn't want to mooch around in fancy hotels. I, too, got jobs in bars. And then I realized Greece had got into my blood and I decided I wanted to read the classics in the original so I studied it at university. I've never regretted it. Even if I hadn't wanted to work here, my life would have been much richer for it. To read Homer in the original is an experience I'd not have missed."

Their drinks came. Rosalie looked into hers, seeing nothing, her mind obsessed with the enigma of the man. He was so tough, so ruthless, and yet so extraordinarily sensitive. So cultured, and at the same time almost brutal. He was watching the fishermen, and the pink pelican who seemed to be a pet, strolling in and out among them. She stole a glance at his clean-cut profile, the iron in him showing in every line of it, in the way he held his head, in the set of his jaw. She must not soften toward him. She must always be on her guard. Don't forget those two beds, audaciously fixed to the floor in one room. The nerve of him! But he had reckoned without the spirit in her. More, considerably more spirit than poor Fay had shown.

"Penny?" As though he had eyes in the back of his head, he swung around and gave her an enigmatic look. She started out of her unhappy reverie. "I was thinking that this job is quite a challenge," she replied truthfully. "I hope I haven't bitten off more than I can chew." He gave her an odd look, penetrating yet cautious, but he did not reply.

Spiro's taverna was in one of the narrow, tightly packed streets in the center of the tiny town. It was intimate, friendly, noisy, and airless. The close-packed tables were covered with snowy white cloths and there were brilliant red napkins by each setting, folded decoratively into the shape of a rose. All around the walls hung fishing nets with a plethora of seashells entwined. Spiro greeted them enthusiastically and with tremendous warmth. "I have kept the best table for you," he told them engagingly. "Come with me. You would be far too hot in here." He led them back to the entrance where a half dozen tables spilled out onto the cobbled square. Blush-pink and golden bougainvillea spilled from the overhang, and there were candles set among the geraniums in little pots on the tables. "It's so pretty," Rosalie exclaimed in delight. "It's like a film set." Spiro looked gratified. They sat down and Spiro went to get a menu. Another pink pelican came wandering past, fixed them with his beady eye, then moved on. "Oh, look," exclaimed

Rosalie, amused, "he's going to jump up on that table."

"It's his own table," said Louis. "He belongs to the restaurant opposite." And indeed he looked very much at home as he tucked his head beneath his wing and went to sleep.

Spiro came swinging back, bright-faced and eager to please. "You would like to inspect the food in the kitchen before you order?" It was a Greek courtesy, Rosalie knew. She was about to push back her chair when Louis said laconically, "The lady has walked far enough today." He glanced down at the menu. "*Dolmádes.* Let's start with that. Then moussaka, and honey cakes to follow." In spite of the fact that Spiro had handed her a copy of the menu, Louis ordered as though he were the only one to be pleased. "Always have ouzo, *dolmádes,* moussaka, and honey cakes the first night." He pronounced moussaka the Greek way: *moo-sar-kar.* Rosalie bit back a protest at his autocratic assumption that she would eat what he wanted. The maddening thing was that it was also what she wanted. "With retsina," he went on imperturbably. "Followed by Greek coffee and Metaxas."

"Provided you're prepared to carry me home," she retorted dryly, swallowing her irritation at his high-handedness. "The local brandy is pretty potent stuff."

"The moussaka will put a good solid lining on your stomach," he replied imperturbably. "I told you, you need to relax."

And she knew it, too. In a curious way she could not help feeling grateful to him for understanding. The *dolmádes* came, delicious little vine-leaf packets of rice and mincemeat, and with them the retsina. Rosalie found herself sparring good-humoredly with Louis, even calling him by his Christian name for the first time without feeling uncomfortable. It was an odd sensation, sitting here with the enemy, trying to dislike him and succeeding only in floating somehow midway between fascination and hate, with a softening at the edges of both so that they seemed to merge. Once, she found herself pondering on what was going to be the outcome of all this and found her mind sheering away.

She must think of the job. It was going to be a challenge and there was nothing she liked better than that. Once they had everything shipshape and the guests were here, the strain of this personal relationship would go, she told herself. Thrown together as they were now, a man and a woman, inevitably there would be emotions involved. With the work contract to fulfill, she could not fall out with him. Neither must she allow herself to come under his spell. Tomorrow, busying herself with what had to be done, she would make certain she did it alone.

For two days the villa complex was a hive of activity. Now that the owner and his executive were actually on the spot the Greeks were galvanized into action. It was true they rose at a daunting hour. Rosalie soon saw she was going to have to either succumb to a siesta after lunch or retire to bed early in order to get enough sleep.

She was wakened on that first morning at break of day by the chatter of workmen. They had come complete with concrete mixer on one of those little trucks Rosalie had seen as they walked along the quay yesterday. Louis, she saw from the front door where she stood in her thin blue cotton pajamas sleepily rubbing her eyes, had cleared the junk and some rough little bushes from the front of the lower villa and had neatly marked out the area that was already flattened and prepared for the terrace. So he was prepared to get down to laboring, too? He was indeed an enigma of a man. He stood in the early-morning light, head and torso bared, his faded jeans taut across a hard stomach, his feet encased in workmanlike boots. Alone, silhouetted against the distant sea, he looked like some Greek god. Or like Pericles, Rosalie thought, leader of ancient Athens.

Angry with herself for even contemplating the unsummoned thought from the hidden reaches of her mind, she swung away and, shooing off the cats that had gathered on the step, went back to bed. But nobody works quietly in Greece. The four workmen sang, shouted, teased, bandied advice back and forth at the tops of their voices, until Rosalie gave up in despair. Solid though the villa walls were, nearly a foot thick in places, they did not keep the noise out. She rose, slipped into jeans and a cotton T-shirt, ran a comb through her hair, took her lists out onto the cool veranda, and set about her work.

At seven-thirty Louis came up the path. He did a double take when he saw her hard at work, head down. "I see I've picked a winner," he said, looking gratified as he advanced with measured tread across the terrace, brown shoulders square, his torso glistening with sweat. At the male smell of him, the sheer animal masculinity, Rosalie caught her breath. He came right up to her and stood looking down at her papers, hands on hips, his well-cut lips parted over magnificent teeth.

"You've picked staff who can't sleep through a friendly Greek chat," she told him wryly.

He grinned. "I'm sorry. What have you got there?"

"Potential menus in this pile," she said, indicating a little sheaf of papers. "A list of everything I can possibly think of for the villas from salt and pepper, pots and pans, to beds. I know you've got everything ordered, but I thought if I start from rock bottom with the empty villas, I've got something to check off and I won't be running around shrieking: 'Heavens alive, he's forgotten the forks!' It's amazing how clear one's head can be when one is starting from scratch. Especially," she added, dimpling, "early in the morning."

"Good girl." He glanced approvingly at her bare feet, the toenails pretty with salmon-colored varnish. "Get yourself into a pair of sandals and I'll escort you to breakfast on the quay. You're going to get some good exercise running up and down this hill for meals until we get shipshape."

"And when we're shipshape, you're going to expect them home-cooked?" she asked, trying him out, watching for a reaction.

"What a suspicious young woman you are," he replied lightly. "Only breakfast, in fact. An intimate little *petit déjeuner* might be pleasant. It was pleasant at the King George, was it not? But, of course, come to think of it, that entails a run to the baker for rolls."

"And cake." She dimpled again.

"No cake," he retorted firmly. "And this morning I'm going to have bacon and eggs, anyway. There's a taverna near the quay that specializes in English breakfasts. You can even get instant coffee if you're plebeian enough to want it. Right, I'll get a shirt." He swung around and in a few long strides was out of sight around the corner.

We're dangerously close to being friends, Rosalie thought apprehensively as she slid her slim feet into brown leather sandals and fastened the buckles. Louis was so extraordinarily easy to get along with at times. He was truly a chameleon. Or a wolf in sheep's clothing, she added to herself. And she knew well enough the sheep's clothing could be off in a flash.

66

They swung off together down the slope and through the narrow early-morning streets of the town where shopkeepers were already putting up their colorful awnings and wheeling stands draped with colorful dresses, scarves, and shawls out onto the pavements. As they came out on the quay the fishing caïques were trailing in after their long night's haul and two pink pelicans, one trailing a broken wing, were treading delicately among the stones as they waited for a little of the catch to come their way. The sun was already warm, almost hot. As they sat down Louis said considerately, "Shade or sun?"

"Sun, please. This will do very well." Rosalie leaned back luxuriously, turning her face up to the sun's rays. "My grandmother was saying I have a perpetual tan, and I did look tanned in England, but really, compared to the locals, I'm pale as a lily. If I'm to be a good advertisement to your package tourists I'd better work on it. What date did you say the first lot arrive?"

"Your grandmother?" Louis queried, bypassing her question and shifting uncomfortably on his seat. He pulled out a packet of cigarettes and lit one, blowing a ring of smoke thoughtfully into the air. "Do you realize that you've never mentioned your family? In fact, do you realize that I don't know a thing about you?" Rosalie felt the hot color rise in her cheeks and turned her head away. "You didn't even give me an honest address."

She started guiltily. "What do you mean?"

"Only that there's no such place as 24 Belsize Avenue, Earls Court," he replied evenly, watching for her reaction as a cat watches, waiting for a mouse to jump.

"You—you—" she floundered. He stopped her from continuing by answering her unspoken accusation. "Oh, yes, I do dare to check up on you. Why do you think I asked for your home address? So that I could get in touch with your next of kin in the event of an accident, of course. It was irresponsible of you to make up an address, Rosalie Darrien, if that's your name. It's a storybook, pretty-pretty kind of name, too. Perhaps that's what made me suspicious, that and the fact that you're as transparent as a piece of tissue paper."

"It is my name," she retorted indignantly, trying to make something of that to put him off the track of what had to be kept secret. At that moment, luckily, the waiter came, a small brown man, white-jacketed, brown-skinned, and with a villainous mustache. "Bacon and two fried eggs," said Louis, "and dry rolls and Nescafé for the lady. You do keep Nescafé for English tourists, I believe?" He ignored her furious glare.

"Yes, sir." The waiter slid away between the tables.

"How dare you order for me? How dare you order me dry rolls and Nescafé when you know perfectly well—" She broke off as he laughed tauntingly.

"One complex reaction deserves another," he replied, his voice light but cutting. "Serves you right. Did you really imagine I came down in the last shower?"

Was the game up already? She could not guess. Those tawny eyes were enigmatic, the hard mouth unreadable. She said hotly, to cover her nervousness, "I didn't ask for the job. You forced it on me. I don't see why I should tell you the story of my life."

"And there's no reason why you shouldn't disappear without a trace, if that's the way you want it," he agreed. "I was just curious, that's all." He reached into his hip pocket and drew out a notebook. "Here's a list of the Darriens in the London phone book.

There aren't many. Which one do you belong to, if it isn't too personal a question?"

She looked down at the firmly stroked writing, the flourishing s's, the wildly crossed t's. His was a hand full of character. She did not need to read the names. There were no Darrien relations in London. And blessedly, her grandmother's name was Oliver.

"My parents are dead," she told him.

"Little orphan Annie," he sneered.

"You could say that," she replied evenly. "My only relative is my grandmother, and she lives outside of London."

"I see. And why is it so important that you keep her identity secret? Have you got something to hide?"

She had indeed got something to hide, she thought grimly. Luckily, before she could think of an answer, the waiter came with his tray and began unloading it. "I'll have Greek coffee," Rosalie said sweetly, handing the cup back to him. "I'm sorry to be a bother, but I've changed my mind. I'll have butter and marmalade too with the rolls."

Infuriatingly, Louis grinned. "It was just a warning," he said. "I like my staff to know where they stand." He tucked into the delicious-smelling bacon and eggs. "Two hours' work on an empty stomach gives a man a good appetite," he commented. "All right, you've got something to hide. I'll accept that. But I warn you that I can be ruthless if I find out there's something underhanded in all this. I don't like employing an anonymous female, however pretty she may be. And I warn you, if I decide I really need to know, I'll find out. There are ways and means."

Of course. Her face suffused with burning color at the thought that he could trace her through her passport number, should he wish. She had made no attempt to shield it from his eyes as they came through passport control at either Heathrow or Athens. Certainly he would find her birth certificate at Somerset House and trace that address to her grandmother, Mrs. Oliver. Fay's name had been Oliver, too. She shivered.

But obviously for the moment he did not feel the matter was crucial. There was time enough to plan what she had to do, providing she did not leave it too long. She must start looking for chinks in his armor. She must formulate a method whereby she could pay him back for what he had done to Fay.

The waiter returned with her Greek coffee and the butter and marmalade she had ordered. They demolished the meal in a strained silence, Louis paid, and in silence still they began the return walk. "I'll go along to the warehouse and shake things up there," Louis said, pausing as they came to a corner, indicating that he was turning left while she should go straight ahead. "I'll have their ears for kebabs if the first consignment of stuff doesn't arrive within the hour." Unexpectedly, in that way he had of catching her off guard, he gripped her hand. "Let's be friends, shall we? I'll grant you that everyone's entitled to a private life." Those lion eyes glimmered down at her and he added softly, "If you'll excuse the Anglo-Saxon expression, I'm just bloody curious, that's all."

Chapter Five

The first consignment of goods did indeed arrive within the hour. It came on one of those little orange-painted trucks, dragging a trailer, and pursued at a leisurely pace by three men pulling a primitive kind of wagon piled precariously with beds. Louis joined the removal men to help with the unloading, and Rosalie, having made her plans for the layout with regard to the number of guests expected, gave orders as to where the furniture was to go. As the sun rose inexorably higher in the sky she sorted out the china and silver, the pots and pans, and worked to make the three villas habitable. They were never going to be attractive inside, she knew, for Greek homes tended to be bare, even a little stark, with their square, boxy rooms and painted walls. At least these three had colorful floor tiles with the familiar and elegant Greek key design in brown, black, and orange.

Perhaps I could get some posters for those blank walls, she thought, standing ruminatively in a doorway, faintly repelled by the purely functional look of the rooms. A wardrobe with drawers. Two beds. A mirror. And that was the lot. I might find some icons. But icons were expensive. She would think of something, she decided.

"Congratulations," she said to Louis, pausing as they met on the rough ground between the upper and middle villas. "You seem to have thought of everything."

"I must give credit where credit is due," he replied, giving her that enigmatic smile. "My secretary was the methodical genius. You met Sylvia in the office. She's a fount of knowledge and a bundle of energy. I'll fly her out later for a treat to see the result of her efforts."

He was so considerate, Rosalie thought, marveling again as she had done a dozen times over the enigma of him. Opportunist, ruffian, and gentleman all within one skin. As the day progressed so did the heat. By midday she felt limp and tired. Her blue cotton T-shirt clung to her damp back and her jeans were wet where they fitted snugly into her waist. A little after one she went to the room she had chosen for herself, a small box at the back of villa number one, removed her damp and rather grubby clothes, and slipped into a yellow bikini. In the bathroom she ran a wet facecloth around her neck under her hair and down between her small breasts. Louis was on the veranda when she emerged. "Trying to start a riot among the concrete mixers?" he asked, looking her over appreciatively.

She dimpled. "I was 'glowing.' I'll slip into camouflage if I have to pass the men." She was well aware that the local girls dressed far more demurely than the

72

tourists and that it was not easy for local men to ignore a display of foreign flesh. Louis pulled out a packet of cigarettes and selected one. Dropping into one of the wooden chairs set around the long table on the terrace, he said, "I could do with a break and you must be whacked."

"I was thinking of taking a siesta after lunch," Rosalie admitted. She glanced at her watch. "I've been on the go for nearly seven hours already. Oh, I'm not complaining," she added as she saw his head come up, the eyes narrowed.

"How about a swim instead? No one works again until late afternoon. Why should we?"

Involuntarily, she clapped her hands in delight. It was one surprise after another with Louis.

"The best sand is on the opposite side of the island at Platiyalos Beach. There are buses going all the time from the square. They take off when they're full. Otherwise, a taxi. Or maybe I could borrow the little truck. If the men are sleeping they won't want it. We can have lunch there and come back about four when it's cooler."

"The very thought of a swim has given me a new lease on life," Rosalie said happily.

"Good. Now let's talk about the next move. I was going down to Spiro's this afternoon to negotiate about meals, but since you're the one who will be dealing with him, perhaps you had better do it. You'll have to negotiate a good price to fit in with the package terms. And you'll have to decide how many meals you're prepared to cook."

He had said there would be six guests to a villa. "For eighteen people? Nineteen counting me." Her heart quailed momentarily, but she brushed the apprehension aside. Of course she could do it.

"You'll have an assistant. Sylvia is finding someone

73

now. She'll be able to cook. And she's to come with the first lot of guests on the twentieth. Don't forget," he added, "Spiro's two aunts will be in each morning to make beds and tidy up. Also to clean up between one batch of guests leaving and the next lot arriving. So as soon as we're shipshape you automatically revert from dogsbody to organizer/hostess/part-time cook and escort, advice giver, first-aid dispenser, and ancient-history buff."

"Is that all?" They laughed together, and Rosalie thought nostalgically how pleasant an interlude this could have been if only things had been different and they could have been friends. Real friends, she amended in her mind, for she was aware they were dangerously close to being friends of a kind now. And *dangerous* was a very fair description of the situation.

They decided to reserve the decision on how many meals the girls would cook until Rosalie found out what kind of bargain she could strike with the taverna. And until she had been to the market and done some cost estimates. "Meantime," said Louis, jumping to his feet in that lithe way he had, "I'll pick up my bathing trunks and a towel." He returned a few moments later to say the men building the terrace were knocking off now for their lunch and siesta and that Angelo, the foreman, would run them to the beach in his little truck.

"That's better than waiting for the bus," said Louis, and Rosalie agreed. She hurried to her room, picked up a pair of thin cotton trousers, and pulled them on over her bikini. Then she added a blouse, picked up her bag and towel, checked that she had a comb and suntan lotion, and hurried out.

They jammed into the front seat with Angelo and roared off up the hill. The steep, narrow road was edged with small, square, white-painted, flat-roofed houses, many of which had pretty dovecotes, spikily decorated, on their roofs. "Look behind you." Louis had to shout over the sound of the engine. She turned to glance through the rear window. Seen from above, the town appeared like a spill of white blocks with apricot-colored tops. They came over the hilltop and the noise of the engine eased. "It's so picturesque. So dramatic," she enthused. "I'm already in love with the island." The close-packed houses had given way now to stone walls, market gardens, a field with a sleepy donkey browsing. "See those buildings with the dome-shaped roofs and raised crosses?" said Louis. "They're chapels. Every family aims to have a chapel of its own, and sometimes through intermarriage, or maybe because they're well off, they have two or three."

He had turned toward her as she looked through the rear window, and now that she straightened herself in the seat he had not edged back. Rosalie was heart-stoppingly aware of his nearness, of the warm, bare torso touching the skin of her arm, but there was no way she could draw apart without coming embarrassingly into contact with the driver. She tried to make her voice brisk, but to her chagrin it sounded breathless, almost shaky, when she spoke. "What a strange, dry landscape. Wild figs, poppies, grapevines, all higgledy-piggledy."

"In such a rocky landscape," Louis replied, "plants grow as and where they can. It's an arid land. Too much sun." A taxi flew past them, raising a cloud of dust. "You'll get grapes, figs, aubergines, tomatoes, and cucumbers easily enough in the market," Louis said. "They come in from these gardens every morning." They sped along the narrow road with its twists and turns, passing carts pulled by donkeys, dashing taxis packed with tourists, black-clad, tired-looking old women with baskets on their heads.

"All the women seem to be under twenty or over seventy here," Rosalie said. "Where are the others?"

Louis' hard mouth turned down and there was an expression of wry sympathy in his eyes. "They're probably the ones you think are over seventy. The peasant women age early in this harsh land. We who are so obsessed by sun should remember it does devastating things to those who toil in it."

"It's a man's country, isn't it!" She was thinking of all those men who played cards hour after hour down on the quay, arguing, drinking their apéritifs. Louis nodded, grinning. "Be careful," she said sharply. "Your chauvinistic side is showing." And be careful yourself, some inner voice warned.

The truck jolted down a long slope to the golden sands and the water. "Oh, what a beautiful beach!" cried Rosalie, her good humor restored in a flash.

It was a wide, curved bay, blue as a cornflower, and bare, with only one or two straggly trees on the point beyond. There were several buildings on the edge of the sand. Restaurants, Rosalie saw now. Louis was speaking to the driver in Greek. "Pick us up as you go back to work," he said. "Thanks." The little truck spun around and bounced off with a roar and clatter of gear-changing. "He's an intrepid driver," Louis acknowledged with a grin. "Well, here we are. A good long swim, then seafood for lunch and a sleep on the sand if you like."

"I couldn't think of anything I'd rather do," Rosalie replied happily, taking to her heels and running across the sand. They dropped their outer garments on the beach, then raced into the glittering sea. It was cool, cold almost by comparison with the heat of the sun, and Rosalie gasped as she plunged under. Louis, with his long strides, was already out in front. She surfaced to see him swimming strongly, straight out into deep water, his arms moving concisely and rhythmically, his feet barely making a splash. I'll bet he does everything well, Rosalie thought, grudgingly admiring. She wished suddenly there was something about him that she could easily despise.

She struck out after him, but neither her speed nor her ability could match his and soon she swung around to float lazily, her face upturned to the sun. A moment later he was there beside her, his black hair gleaming, those thick lashes heavy with salt water. "Race you." Though Rosalie was a good swimmer she was no match for him. They swam, dived, cavorted pleasurably until they were breathless, then turned on their backs and floated, the sun hot on their faces. There might have been nobody in the water, nobody on the beach, for all they were aware in those halcyon moments.

Louis said forcefully, "I'm starving," and rolling over added: "Race you to the shore." They splashed out, shaking the salt water from their hair. Then suddenly she misjudged a step in the knee-deep water, tripped, and fell. His hand shot out quick as a flash, supporting her. She looked up with a gasp and their eyes met. For one moment there was heaven in that look, and then suddenly her heart began to pound with fear. She snatched her hand away.

"What shall it be?" asked Louis lightly, looking straight out in front. "Lobster?" And she knew that he, too, had felt something. Something that crushed with velvet feet all petty human thoughts of revenge, hate, anger. Something as deep as fate, and as inevitable. Something beyond desire.

They went across the hot sands toweling themselves

dry, picked up their outer garments and draped them over their arms, slid their toes into sandals. Their brief bathing gear was virtually dry by the time they reached the restaurant a bare two hundred yards away. They sat at a table that was half shaded by a striped awning.

They shared a lobster. Snow-white meat against a glowing vermilion shell. And there was the inevitable Greek salad of olives, tomatoes, cucumbers, and herbs drenched in olive oil.

"Retsina?"

Rosalie asked lightly, not daring to meet his eyes, "Do you want me to concentrate this afternoon, or not?"

"You'll work it off swimming." He signaled the waiter. They ate in silence, poignantly aware of the chatter going on around them, and gradually the awkwardness that had arisen from the heightened sexuality between them fell away. They swam again and briefly they both did fall asleep on the sun-hot sands, their heads pillowed by a towel, their fingers and toes caressed by the silky, shifting grains of sand.

Suddenly it was four o'clock and the little truck was on the road above them, its driver noisily signaling his arrival with the strident horn.

"Am I really getting paid for this?" Rosalie murmured sleepily as she dragged herself to her feet and prepared to face the second half of the day.

"You'll feel you've earned it by the time you've faced up to the arguments about catering with young Spiro," Louis retorted wryly. "I hope you've got some Scots blood in you and can strike a hard bargain. And talk to him in Greek so he has no excuse to say later he didn't understand."

"Why don't you do it yourself?" she asked with spirit, feeling that perhaps he was better equipped.

"Because if I set everything up for you, then run off back to London and leave you to cope, he'll take advantage of you because the boss is away. If you're seen to be the boss from the start, then he won't feel impelled to try any tricks. Spiro is a wily man, and if you want to keep on top you'd best remember that."

She frowned. "I thought you said Spiro was your partner. Why do I have to spar with him over prices?" Louis looked at her reprovingly but did not answer, and she remembered with an uprush of embarrassment that Spiro's "partnership" was a complex one forged by this hardheaded businessman to ease his way in a foreign country. And he had the nerve to call Spiro wily, she thought, smarting from his critical look because she had briefly forgotten something he told her. He had a nerve!

Louis opened the door of the little truck and they slipped in beside the driver for the ten-minute journey back to the villas.

For her first foray into local business Rosalie changed into her neat white trousers and a straight jacket. "Very sensible," said Louis, looking her over approvingly. "No cleavage, no curves. That's the way to look when you're talking business with a susceptible Greek."

She dimpled. "Is Spiro so susceptible?"

"There was never a Greek born who was more susceptible to women," replied Louis. "Well, best of luck."

Rosalie emerged from her foray very gratified. She hurried back to the complex two hours later, eager to impart her news. As she came up the hill toward the windmill she saw Louis, torso bared to the sun, setting up a framework for the vines that had been tumbled to the ground when the way was cleared for the concrete terrace. There's one thing about him, she

79

thought, again with grudging admiration, he's prepared to work as hard as his employees! He lifted his head, saw her, and left what he was doing to come forward and meet her. "How did it go?"

She bit back the excitement bursting in her. This was job satisfaction at its best. "Come and sit down and I'll give you the comparative figures," she suggested. She chased the cats off the terrace, and Louis and she sat down at the big table. "I've got a sheaf of menus, priced. And on another sheet I'll show you the bargain I've struck. It was quite a battle, but I think we're both satisfied. Spiro gets eighteen people for a guaranteed four nights a week and three to five lunches, to be adjusted after the first batch of guests go when I've found my feet and discovered how much free time I'll have for preparation and marketing. Also," she added, "when I see the caliber of the assistant you're sending out. If she's energetic and willing it will be easier. So don't choose her for her looks, if you can help it."

"I always choose staff for their looks." He grinned.

"You said your secretary was to choose her, come to think of it," Rosalie retorted.

"I have the final say. She's sorting the wheat from the chaff. I like to make the final decision."

She glared at him. "Then don't forget to ask her if she can cook." There was a mischievous look in his eyes that made her apprehensive, and she had an uncomfortable feeling it was not totally for the reason that nineteen guests were a lot of people to cook for.

That night after dinner at Spiro's they walked through the town. The streets, magnificent with bougainvillea and geraniums trailing under lamplight over white-painted stone walls, were gay with laughter and hurrying feet. "There's a nightclub of sorts somewhere here," Louis remarked. "Do you feel like listening to Greek music?"

"How lovely." They turned a corner and there was the melancholy sound of a bouzouki faintly on the air.

Louis was wearing one of those silk shirts in which he looked so well, the front unbuttoned to reveal his muscled chest, the golden-brown color of it seeming to match and highlight his eyes. His dark glossy hair fell carelessly across his brown forehead. "Come on," he said, taking her arm and leading her toward a little blue doorway slightly below the level of the street.

It was dark inside, the room only faintly lit by low-watt bulbs concealed in shells on walls and ceiling. There were fishing nets strewn across corners in a haphazard yet decorative way and geraniums growing prettily out of pots on the tables. They sat down close by a window, for it was very hot. Rosalie was wearing an Indian blouse of fine lawn, flower patterned, with a soft neckline and loose flowing sleeves. She wore a red frilly skirt that matched and had tied the two together with a twist of multicolored cord that accentuated her small waist. Louis ordered Greek coffee. "Brandy?" Rosalie demurred, but he ordered it all the same. "Two Metaxas, if you please." Then to Rosalie: "When in Rome do as the Romans do. Do you know any of the Greek dances, by the way?"

"Yes. A little. I learned one or two on Corfu."

"Great. You know the men like to dance by themselves—this being a chauvinistic country, as you've already pointed out—but we English can ignore the rules. They're too courteous to object."

The drummers were playing softly. Now the man with the bouzouki joined in. Two men got up to dance, and Louis drew Rosalie to her feet. "Let's see how good you are."

But it was Louis who was good. For so big a man he was extraordinarily light on his feet and he knew the steps to perfection. The music grew faster and faster. Others joined them on the floor; two of the waiters, carried away by the heady strains of the big guitarlike instrument, swung a cloth off one of the tables and jumped up to dance on it. Presently the whole room was alive with leaping and shouting, with tapping feet and whirling skirts. Some German tourists had come in and were shouting "Bravo!" and clapping their hands. Wilting, Rosalie went back to the table as the music stopped. Her hair was wild about her head, her cheeks scarlet. Louis, laughing, pushed up the window. "Let's have some air. So you know Greek dancing 'a little'?" he mocked her. "How good are you when you know something well, mystery girl?"

She smiled, pretending not to notice he had resurrected the conflict between them, though her heart had begun to beat a little faster. "You're very kind. You're no slouch yourself."

"Here's your coffee. But concentrate on the Metaxas."

It just might loosen my tongue, she thought. That's what he means. At some time he was going to learn about her relationship to Fay. But not yet, she vowed. Not until she had found a way to pay him back. She lifted the glass to her lips. It was softer than the French brandy, but unaccustomed to hard liquor as Rosalie was, she felt it catch at her throat. "It's nice," she said politely, her eyes smarting. But if he supposed he was going to get her to drink more, she thought suspiciously, then he would be disappointed.

They danced again, and as Rosalie swung from one partner to another, arms held high in a precision movement, she saw Louis from a new angle, towering head and shoulders over the Greeks, his hair as dark

and as luxuriant, his skin golden by comparison with
the dark skins around him, a lusty, vigorous young
god, and she was reminded again of the ancient
Greeks, of Apollo, god of the sun. She lost Louis then
as she danced her way in and out of the lively throng,
swinging close against a broad Greek chest, springing
away to take the hand of a blond German tourist,
moving in a chain from hand to hand. Then Louis was
suddenly confronting her, his lean, cool hands on her
fingers, and to her chagrin she knew her heart beat a
little faster as she swept by. When the music stopped
she was on the opposite side of the room to her table.
A handsome Greek with whom she found herself
looked at her admiringly, his dark eyes on a level with
hers, his warm hands caressing her forearms. "You
are alone?"

She smiled politely. "No. I am with a man."

"Oh. Is a pity." He shrugged, offering his arm. "To
your man, then." And he escorted her through the
dispersing crowd across the floor. As they approached
the table Louis was pressing something into a waiter's
hand. He looked up. "Ah! There you are." Nodding
cursorily to her escort, he pulled out her chair. "Do
drink up," he said as she took her place.

She glanced down at the brandy and obligingly took
a sip. Odd, she seemed not to have touched it. The
fat, bulbous glass appeared still to have a full measure. She must not appear to be rude. Louis was being
generous. And after all, this Metaxas was sweeter and
softer than the brandy she had had at other times. Not
so bad at all, especially taken sip for sip with the
delicious coffee.

As the evening progressed tourists and locals
poured into the nightclub until it seemed it must
stretch at the seams to accommodate them all. The
band played louder and, it seemed, faster. A guitarist

had come to join the group, and another drummer, swelling the sound until the walls rang with music. Rosalie, occasionally sipping her brandy, began to feel lightheaded. It was nearly three o'clock in the morning when the tempo changed. More men leaped onto the tables and these were holding plates in their hands.

Louis grasped her wrist, jerking Rosalie to her feet. "They're starting the rough stuff. It's a peculiarly Greek tradition—throwing plates. Let's get out of here." Already there was the crash of splintering china as plates were hurled against the walls.

They turned toward the door, but it was blocked by a laughing mob. Some other dancers were trying to get past and the crowd was jammed solid. Louis swung around. "Through the window. Come on." They ran back to the table, flung their legs over the sill, and dropped. But the ground outside was not, as they had anticipated, on a level with the one they had left. Louis lost his balance, gave a warning yell, and toppled into a mass of bougainvillea. It was too late to stop. Rosalie had already thrown her weight forward. With a cry she fell on top of him in a tangle of arms and legs, leaves and blossoms. His arms came out and around her, holding her tightly.

In the fall her blouse had come loose and swung up over her face, blinding her, exposing her small breasts confined within a narrow lace bra. In a wild, exotic moment she felt his lips on the curve of her bosom. Instinctively, her fingers tightened on his lean, hard shoulders. There was a heady smell of sweat and blossom, and mustiness from the soil. She relaxed against him, her head spinning, lips parted, a great rush of warmth and generosity welling up and spreading through her. She could feel the long, lean length of him beneath her and her errant heart gloried in its nearness. He moved and she slipped into the curve of his arm. He lowered her blouse from her face and with heart-stopping gentleness his lips met hers. Something fired through her at his touch, some savagery she did not know she possessed and could not control. She clung to him, and as though he only awaited the signal, his own passion broke loose.

Heaven alone knew what would have happened then, she thought afterward in the sober light of dawn, but that there was a rush of feet on the cobblestone path overhead, accompanied by cries of dismay as the young people jostled one another in their breakaway from the door. The raucous sounds brought reason to Rosalie's fevered brain and she fought her way out of Louis' arms to sit up, disheveled and panting, in the frail moonlight.

Louis, too, had pulled himself to a sitting position. He reached out one hand and tenderly touched her bruised cheek. It was an exquisite moment, just before sanity returned. And then someone leaned over the little wall above crying in distress: "They've fallen down there—those people who went through the window. Can we help?"

Rosalie's head was spinning as willing hands helped them up. There was anxiety, then laughter. "These wild Greeks."

"It happens all the time. The traditional plate smashing . . . Once it starts, there's no holding them."

"Are you all right?"

At last they were free of the helpful, noisy, excited throng, hurrying along the narrow streets between the little boxlike, white-painted houses, keeping at arm's length from each other, Rosalie painfully sensitive to Louis' nearness. As they went up the hill where the picturesque windmill stood outlined against the dawn he accidentally brushed her hand. Rosalie jumped as though at the sound of a pistol shot. Suddenly he grasped her hand and swung her around to face him. "Well," he demanded, "are you going to pretend it didn't happen?" She tried to jerk her hand away, but he had it in a grip like steel.

Suddenly she knew, or thought she knew, what had happened. "You had my brandy topped up," she flared at him accusingly. "I saw you tipping the waiter. You got me d-dr-drunk—so I didn't know what was happening. How dare you, you—you—you unprincipled . . ."

"Scoundrel is probably the word you're searching for," Louis said coldly, his eyes like smoldering steel in the lamplight. He thrust her hand violently from him as though it hurt him. "If that's what you want to think, then go on thinking it, but I'll tell you this, nymph, people tend to behave more true to their natures when they've had one over the eight."

"Eight!" she flared. "You had it filled eight times while my back was turned?"

He laughed harshly. "One over the eight is a saying," he said scathingly. He stepped closer, his eyes burning down into hers. "And just in case you need the advice, I'm warning you, I'm a man with all a man's instincts. If you think you're playing with an inexperienced—"

She cut him off ruthlessly because she was in a panic. He was too close, too immeasurably powerful. His sexuality was a beacon in the night. "I'm not playing at all."

He gripped her hand again, moved it closer to him so that she felt the warm flesh of his bare chest against her knuckles. "Aren't you?" he asked softly. "Are you really not? I'd advise you to look into the truth of what you say because this"—he lowered his lips inexorably to taste hers again at his leisure—"is a very small sample of what I can do when roused." She stared back up at those black-lashed eyes like a small creature of the woods mesmerized in the headlamps of a car, unable to break away, her lower lip caught between her teeth, her heart thumping. And then suddenly he let her go. She was free and somehow walking up the final slope to the brow of the hill where the villas lay, her head spinning, her mind telling her to run, and run, and never stop until she had her bags packed and was safely aboard a plane for England.

Chapter Six

She was dreaming. She was sitting on the edge of a ravine with her legs dangling over and Louis was on the other edge, watching her, reaching across, then retreating, frustrated by her inaccessibility. Yet there was a way across the ravine to her side. She knew about it, and she wanted to tell him how to cross, but someone with a strange devil's body and Fay's angelic face kept saying "No, you mustn't." She woke with a start as a weight seemed to crash on her feet. Her eyes flew open to see Louis had seated himself on the end of her bed.

"I thought you might not want to sleep through lunch," he said.

"What!" Horrified, Rosalie leaped into a sitting position. She glanced at her watch. "One o'clock! Heavens! Why didn't you wake me?"

"If the concrete mixers didn't wake you, then I reasoned you needed the sleep," he replied, then added in that way he had of splintering a kindness, "I also reasoned that a droopy assistant yawning and making mistakes wasn't going to be much use to me. There's quite a lot of hard work to be done this afternoon. Swimming's off the schedule."

"Of course," she agreed, rubbing her eyes, suddenly conscious of the loose, low-necked pajama top she wore and the way her blond hair was tumbled around her head. "I'm terribly sorry. I really am."

"I'll forgive you," he replied magnanimously, and she found herself flushing because there seemed more to his offer than was warranted by the error of oversleeping. "There's a plumber coming later to fix that awkward tap in the kitchen," he told her, "and if you wouldn't mind shifting your beautiful body into less diverting gear, I'd like a hand with the vine. I've got the trellis in place now, and Spiro has provided a ladder, but I need someone to sort out the trailers and hand them up to me."

As soon as Louis had gone Rosalie jumped out of bed, slid under the not-so-cold shower, and afterward pulled on her working jeans and a bright yellow T-shirt. She found Louis sorting the long strands of bougainvillea that had been torn from the villa walls when space had been cleared for the terrace. It was a long job, inevitably made slow because the concrete was still wet and had to be carefully avoided. It was nearly two o'clock and very hot when they finished. Rosalie, hungry, was beginning to wonder if Louis intended that she should have nothing to eat at all. Then he said, "Shoot down to Spiro's, will you, and have a spot of lunch."

"What about you?" With one hand resting on a slim hip, she brushed damp strands of hair wearily back from her forehead.

89

"I haven't really got time. Get Spiro to give you a plate of moussaka."

"And bring it back here? Oh, no, really. You must have a break," Rosalie protested.

"I rang London this morning," he told her. "There are one or two complications with my affairs. I'm going to have to go back in three days' time and leave you holding the fort. If you don't want to make it too difficult for yourself," he added in that quicksilver way he had of changing from urbane to bleak, "you'll bring the moussaka. Spiro will protest, of course. No Greek eats on the job. But you can manage him if you put your mind to it."

He's giving me a bit of advice, Rosalie thought as she hurried off down the slope and into the town. He's telling me I'm to be the boss when he goes. Hadn't he implied Spiro was merely a partner to ease an Englishman's way with the authorities? Louis was crafty to the fingertips, she thought bleakly, remembering again why she was here and, with a sense of inadequacy, what she had to do.

Spiro met her with a flourish of a snow-white napkin. "You have come to lunch alone, Miss Darrien? Where is my friend Louis?"

She glanced around the tables that stood on the cobblestoned square, hoping she would not have to go inside where the atmosphere was oppressive. "I'm afraid it's my fault, Spiro," she told him ruefully. "We went dancing last night and I overslept. Now we're behind with the work and Louis is having to pay. Please, could I be served quickly? I don't mind what I eat so long as it comes immediately. And a plate of moussaka to take back."

"For Louis?" He was, as Louis had surmised, amazed, and rather shocked. "How can you carry a plate of moussaka, Miss Darrien?"

"Quite easily," she told him briskly. "Just put it in some sort of box."

"Lunch in a box," growled Spiro in disgust, flouncing off to the kitchen as Rosalie sat down. But he did Louis proud. When she had finished her *tyrópitta,* that delectable cheese pie with marjoram, a waiter arrived with a big box containing not only the moussaka ordered but also a cucumber and olive salad, the ubiquitous crème caramel, and half a bottle of retsina.

"Tell him it must not happen again," said Spiro, looking distressed. "Louis must not work so hard."

"I'll tell him. And thank you very much." She gave him her sweetest smile, said goodbye, and hurried back through the narrow streets. She took the hill as fast as she could. Louis saw her coming, put the ladder away, and was already seated impatiently at the veranda table with fork in hand when she arrived. Lusty. Aggressive. Taking what he wanted when he wanted it, the graces discarded, masculinity and healthy strength uppermost. Masculinity! She caught her upper lip between her teeth. Louis was the most masculine man she had ever known. The male vibrations thrilled out toward her, setting up a tingling sensation in her nerves as he attacked the moussaka with lusty appetite.

"I'll fetch you a glass," she said. "And a spoon." She added lightly, "Like it or not, you've got crème caramel."

"I love crème caramel," he retorted with his mouth half full. "Just at the moment I could eat an ox, I believe, rib by rib."

She frowned, immediately concerned. "You missed breakfast, didn't you?" Perhaps waiting for me to wake up, she thought guiltily. He would do that?

"I was busy," he replied casually. "By the way"—he pointed the fork at her, and she thought

with amusement that the gesture from anyone else
would have been decidedly rude, but his unique vigor
transcended even bad manners—"there were four
pubs in a row."

"Where?" she asked, puzzled by the sudden switch
of subject.

"In England, of course. Fellows used to have a
drink in each pub in turn. Then they'd go back to the
first and do the row again. The average chap could
carry that amount of liquor, eight glasses. If they
failed to go home after that, and went back to the first
pub, and got drunk, it was said they had 'one over the
eight.'"

"Thank you," she replied demurely, the color
flaring in her cheeks. "I'm sorry about last night."

"Don't be sorry. I always suspected you were a
flesh-and-blood woman. A man likes to be proved
right." Not knowing what to say, she turned and went
swiftly into the villa. Perhaps it was as well Louis was
returning to England.

The three days following were busy in the extreme.
Spiro produced a cousin called Nicholas—as lively
and sparkling, as slim-hipped and handsome, as
himself—who was willing to take the guests out in his
brightly painted caïque. Rosalie negotiated a price.
Each day, somehow, they found time for a swim. Of
her own volition, Rosalie opened an account with the
beach restaurant at Platiyalos, battling with the pro-
prietor for a fair price on a long-term basis. Greek
prices were low compared with costs in England, but
she knew she had to watch closely, for Louis had
given her the cost figures and the profit needed to
make the business stand on its own feet. It was a
challenge to make the scheme not only work, but
work well.

She knew now that Louis was no average travel

agent, as she had at first thought. His interests were wide and varied. There was a property-development company in London, and he had an estate in the Home Counties that was being run rather extravagantly by his brother-in-law. "I let him have it for my sister's sake," Louis had told Rosalie, "and very much against my business judgement. Sometimes I wake up in the cold light of morning thinking I'll sack him; then I remember what a hard time my sister would have if left entirely at his mercy, and I weaken. He's a charming chap, but like a good many charmers, he's feckless. He'd rather ride at point-to-points on expensive horses than see to the new lambs in a hailstorm."

I wonder if Louis knows how much charm he exudes himself, she asked herself. But feckless he certainly was not. She had not known about his loyalty before. There was something to learn of this strange man every day. But she never allowed herself to forget how he had treated Fay, and she tried not to forget, as it was so easy to do, why she had come and what she had set herself to do. It was not easy to think of something that would strike at the heart of this man. He had a boldness, a hardiness, that she knew deep inside her would smash any tentative little plan of hers to smithereens and leave him laughing. There was one way to get at him, she knew, and sometimes in the reaches of the night she considered it, breathlessly, but when the cold light of dawn came she was afraid. Afraid of herself? She thrust the admission away.

It was curious, that empty feeling when he had gone. Georges Mixiades, the builder, ran Louis to the airport in his rattling little truck. Waving goodbye, Rosalie suppressed a smile as she realized Louis was equally at home in the vehicle that transported the concrete mixer as he had been in the glamorous King

George Hotel. She went back to her work feeling oddly lost. The villa, too, though she had in fact been the sole occupant each night, seemed empty, as though it had lost its heart.

I'll enjoy being on my own, she told herself crisply. But as dinnertime approached and she contemplated the walk down into town she felt oddly forlorn. She went into her room and opened the new built-in wardrobe that Spiro's cousin—one of his many cousins—had erected. She had not brought many dresses; there were only three to choose from, but each looked quite unsuitable for a dinner alone. In the end she slipped into white linen trousers and a tailored burnt-sienna blouse. She ran a comb carelessly through her hair, smoothing back the tendrils that always gathered softly around her face. She could not be bothered taking the elastic band off and brushing her hair loose. Who was going to look at her, anyway?

Too many men, she discovered to her annoyance, now that she had no escort. Not feeling hungry, she wandered down to the quay. A cruise ship had been in that day and the passengers were now piling back into the little launches that would return them to their seagoing hotel. Absently, Rosalie pulled out a chair and sat down at one of the taverna tables to watch the animated scene. Fishermen in their black peaked caps were busily preparing their caïques for a night on the water. The tame pelicans trod delicately up and down on the white-ringed cobblestones.

"Me-ees! You are alone? I join you?" A smiling, black-haired young man had already drawn out the chair opposite. "You are very preetty, mees."

She flushed and told him bleakly to go away.

"But you are alone and I am alone," he pointed out cajolingly. "Why not we have a drink together?"

"Because I don't want to drink with you," she

94

retorted in Greek. She had not meant to snap like that. She turned her back. But he stayed, wheedling plausibly with a silken tongue until it was she who rose and left. She was approached three times on the short walk to Spiro's restaurant. She arrived pink-faced and despairing, illogically angry with Louis for leaving her. Local girls were always with their families, she knew. There was no getting near them until at least an engagement, if not a marriage, was arranged. A Greek girl's virginity was her marriage ticket. She would not attract an eligible suitor without it. So the foreigners had to suffer the pressing attentions of the men. "Don't blame them," she had advised irritated newly arrived tourists more than once when she was working at the bars in Corfu and Kos. "They're randy because they're frustrated by circumstances." But tonight she did blame them. I've lost my sense of humor all of a sudden, she told herself, trying hard to smile. I'd better work at getting it back.

The next day and the next went slowly in spite of the fact that there was a lot of work to do. Depressed by the bareness of the villa now that she was alone, she went into the town and bought some bright tiles and flowerpots. Down on the quay she persuaded an old fisherman to give her a pretty yellow net that was beyond repair, and then she searched the pebbly section of the beach below the windmill for shells. That evening she amused herself draping the net attractively across the front of the villa where she slept and adorning it with the shells she had found. Then she fixed the tiles on the white front walls of the other villas and, digging up some blue campanula and wild iris, potted them and set the pots prettily around the terraces. The villas had a lived-in look now, she decided with satisfaction. She wondered if Louis would be pleased.

On the third day, feeling cut off and lonely, she introduced herself to some young tourists, who invited her to join them for a meal. She did not know what had happened to her normally independent spirit. She had never been lonely like this before. Even when she first came to Greece, after that unfortunate clash when Fay had gone off with Stephen, she had enjoyed her exile and the diversions it offered. Now she found herself becoming moody. She had to fight the blues off. She rose early these mornings, walking down to the little bay directly over the hilltop from the villas where the white windmill lay and around the point from the town. Here, though the water was not nearly so attractive as that at the beach on the opposite side of the island, she could have a perfectly adequate swim. There was a hotel here and sometimes she was joined by tourists who preferred the sea to the swimming pool.

"Water like wine," Louis had said quoting from Homer's *Iliad*. She pushed thoughts of Louis away when they came into her mind, as they did all too frequently. It was only because she was lonely, she told herself. She was looking forward to the company of the first batch of guests.

Louis had been gone a week. The little villa complex was fast becoming shipshape. The new concrete terraces were dry and hard; the bougainvillea that overhung the middle one had recovered from its ordeal and was drooping luxuriantly across the new frame as though it had been there forever. Comfortable cane chairs, locally made and ordered months ago, had arrived at last and Rosalie had placed them on the lower terraces. She had found some tiny square tables in a junkyard at the back of the town, had them repaired, and painted them in the hard Greek colors that the fishermen used on the caïques. Ocher, brick,

Silhouette Romance

JANET DAILEY
The Hostage Bride

CAROLE HALSTON
Love Legacy

DONNA VITEK
Veil of Gold

NANCY JOHN
Outback Summer

4 Free Book Certificate

Mail Today to Reserve Your Home Subscription

Silhouette Romance

P.O. Box 910 Stratford, Ontario N5A 6W3

YES, please send me <u>FREE</u>, and without obligation, the 4 exciting Silhouette paperback originals described in this offer. Unless you hear from me after I receive my <u>4 FREE</u> books, please send me 6 full-length, Silhouette Romances to preview each month, as soon as they are published. I understand that each month you will bill me just $1.75 each (a total of $10.50) with *no additional shipping, handling or other hidden charges.* There is no minimum number of books that I must buy, and I can cancel this arrangement anytime I wish. The first 4 books are mine to keep, even if I never take a single additional book.

Signature _____
(if under 18, parent or guardian must sign)

Name _____

Address _____

City _____

Prov. _____ Code _____

4 FREE BOOKS NOW . . .
6 BOOKS EVERY MONTH
Delivered Right to Your Own Home

This offer limited to one per household, expires July 31, 1983. If price changes are necessary you will be notified.

WE PAY THE POSTAGE ... SEE OVER

C1-55-383

Printed in Canada

MAIL TO-DAY AND RECEIVE
4 SILHOUETTE ROMANCES
FREE! (A $7.80 value)

red, and green. They gave her own terrace a festive, lively look. One evening as she sat looking out over the shimmering sea where the sun was going down she felt inexpressibly lonely. So lonely it was almost painful. As darkness fell she sighed, rose, and went to the newly painted kitchen. But there was nothing there she fancied eating. Unable to face another meal alone, she went to bed.

There was only one day to go now and the first batch of tourists would arrive. Rosalie went down to the post office with her passport as she did every day to see if there was any mail and found a letter from her grandmother. Mrs. Oliver wrote agitatedly: "I've got some rather uncomfortable news for you, dear. Stephen came to see me not long after you had gone. Naturally, I told him where you were and what you were doing. I didn't actually tell him Mr. Alexander's name, but he said straightaway, 'That's Aegean Villas Inc., isn't it?' Apparently he had seen their advertisements. As you probably know, there has been a big advertising campaign. I thought for one awful moment he knew the father of the baby was Louis Alexander, but evidently he didn't. Then today he arrived again at my door, smiling all over his face. It seems he had made inquiries about going to Mykonos, found the whole summer already booked, and put himself on a waiting list for a cancellation. Now . . ."

Rosalie did not have to read any further. Stephen, who had unwittingly given his name to Louis and Fay's stillborn love child, was on his way with the first lot of guests! She sat on a low stone wall at the side of the street that ran down to the sea and stared blindly before her.

Certainly Louis might not have known Fay's married name, for she had reverted, at Stephen's angry request, to her maiden name of Oliver. But it only needed Stephen to remark, "I was married briefly to Rosalie's stepsister," and mention her name, to create an intolerable situation. Louis was far too bright to let that pass. By the same token, one slip of the tongue, one staggered look from Louis, and Stephen might guess that Louis was the man who, through letting Fay down, had involved him in his distressing and disastrous marriage. It must not happen. And yet how could she stop Stephen from coming?

Rosalie toyed frantically with the wording of telegrams. DON'T COME. I AM RETURNING. But she could not return. And anyway, such a message might not put Stephen off. If he had wanted a holiday on a Greek island, if her presence had merely been the trigger to his decision, then he would come anyway. DON'T COME. WRITING. No, that would not do either, for inevitably she would have to explain in the letter. And she could not, must not, tell Stephen. He must never know the name of the man behind the outrage he had suffered. Besides, if he was actually coming to see her, then his presence would be uncomfortable and embarrassing for them both. How could she love a man who had once let her down and then, adding insult to injury, married her stepsister?

"Oh, what a mess!" she groaned. "What an inflammable, diabolical mess." One of those mangy cats that bothered her so much had settled on the cobblestones and was gazing up into her face. She looked away.

That evening Rosalie paced up and down the quay, a prey to fears and apprehensions, racking her mind to think of a way out. But there was none. Stephen was going to turn up and there was nothing, absolutely nothing, she could do about it. She made a mental note to put him in villa number two. At least if Louis remained in three that kept them all apart. She hoped grimly that the new assistant, or one of the guests, might be attracted to Stephen, but in her heart she knew it was not going to be as simple as that.

The next day dragged miserably. Stephen and Louis, Stephen and Louis, Rosalie kept thinking, thrown together on a Greek island. And both men, in a fringe way, with the same interests. Property. They would have plenty to discuss together. They could easily become friends, until . . . Would Louis know Stephen's home address? Was Louis likely to peruse the guest list? Or did the secretary called Sylvia deal with names and addresses on her own? By midafternoon when the plane was due she was sick with apprehension. Louis' voice rang in her ears: "So you come from Cataran? I knew a girl, now dead, who lived there." She shuddered.

The taxis drew up one behind the other in front of the first villa. The other two villas were reached by a little trail of steps edged prettily with the golden daisies and variegated rock plants that grew so easily in the dry, stony soil. Louis jumped out of the first car, his strong face alight, for all the world as though he were one of the holidaymakers, Rosalie thought as she came unhappily down off the terrace to meet them.

"Everything okay, nymph?" He saw the bright tables and chairs, the draped golden net and the shells. "My! What a transformation!" His face softened and he looked at her with a new, warm expression in his eyes. With something like gratitude and respect.

"Everything's fine." But she said it through stiff lips and her knees were trembling. "I'm glad you like the decor." Then she turned quickly to the new arrivals. They poured out of the taxis, laughing girls in jeans and colorful blouses with pale skins and expectant, glowing faces. Men, bright-eyed, curious, affable, looked around with pleased expressions.

"Lovely spot! So you're the hostess. I'm Brian."

"I'm Felicity."

And then, carrying his own bag in that quiet, responsible, typical way, Stephen Barrington walked calmly through the group right up to Rosalie and, taking her hands, kissed her warmly on both cheeks. "Hello, Ro," he said, smiling. "Surprised?"

Something, some force Rosalie could not resist, was dragging her head around. Her apprehensive eyes met Louis' golden ones, unreadable behind their sooty lashes. With immense aplomb he remarked lightly, "Instant friends?"

Stephen turned to him. "We're old chums," he said innocently in his nice way.

"Right," snapped Louis, addressing the crowd, "allow me to introduce Rosalie. She's your hostess and her job is to make your stay as comfortable as she possibly can. Anything you want, ask her." And then he added, his voice double-edged but light, his eyes glinting, "She's on duty twenty-four hours a day!"

Stephen, looking slightly taken aback, asked, "Does that mean you can't—"

Rosalie broke in nervously. "I shan't be able to spend time with you, Stephen. I hope you didn't expect me to. I'm here on a job, not a holiday." Looking uncertain, a little crushed, he picked up his bag once more.

"You're in that villa," Rosalie said, pointing to the one that lay immediately below and smiling kindly at him, though her heart was thumping with apprehension. He went away with the others and Rosalie turned to see Louis coming forward arm in arm with a startlingly beautiful girl. She was taller than Rosalie.

Her jet-black hair lay in a sweeping curve across her high forehead. Her mouth was delicate, only faintly touched with lipstick, and she had big, limpid gray eyes. Rosalie's first reaction was one of utter dismay. She had to prevent herself from exclaiming, "You're not the new assistant!" This girl looked as though she had never lifted a hand to help herself. Her nails were rose-colored, long, and beautifully kept. Her elegantly cut cream linen trousers fitted like a second skin and she wore a sleeveless suede jerkin that must have cost the earth. Her already overlong legs were extended by high spiked heels that were totally unsuitable for traversing the rough, stony paths between the villas.

"Allow me to present Janine Cavendish," Louis said smoothly. "Janine is your new assistant. Don't be deceived by looks," he added, his eyes roving admiringly over the other girl from head to bare, rose-tinted toenails. "She assures me she's tough, resilient, hardworking, and utterly responsible."

"Hello, you're Rosalie," the new girl purred in just the kind of voice, Rosalie thought bitterly, she would have expected her to have.

"I'm assuming you two will want to be in separate villas so as to make yourselves easily available to the greatest number of guests," Louis went on smoothly, "so I've arranged for Janine to sleep in the lower villa."

"I'm sure that will be very convenient," Rosalie retorted in a hollow voice and only just stopped herself from adding scathingly, "With you, of course." She turned away. "I'd better see how the guests are sorting themselves out." She was seething as she went from room to room asking the young people if there was anything they wanted and seeing that they were settled comfortably. How typical of

Louis to bring a girl like that! "I hope you weren't expecting luxury," she said to them, forcing herself to smile. "Greek villas, even the private ones, tend to be bare. Board or tiled floors, white-painted walls. It's a picturesque country, but it's stark in the extreme."

None of them, it seemed, had been to Greece before. "So I must warn you about the plumbing." She smiled, feeling as though her face would crack with the strain. "They're old villas, as you see, walls a foot thick and with small windows to keep out the glare, but they've been completely done over. However, the plumbing is never quite adequate, so don't take fright if water oozes up through the grate in the bathroom floor, or if you suddenly find the taps are dry. On top of the hill the water pressure fluctuates. But we think the view is worth a bit of climbing and an occasional inconvenience." She bit her lips. Whom did she mean by "we"? Louis and her?

The guests pronounced themselves ecstatic. "It's nice for you to have a friend in the first batch of guests," said a girl called Nan. "I sat with Stephen Barrington on the plane and he told me you were engaged once. It's great that you can get together again."

Rosalie's response was electric. "I never was engaged to him," she flared.

The girl blinked in surprise, looking somewhat taken aback at Rosalie's violent reaction. "Why would he say that, then?"

"I knew him. But we weren't engaged."

"Oh, I see." The girl chuckled knowingly. "That's better. Then there won't be any traumas. You're just getting together again."

"We're not getting together again," Rosalie said distinctly. "It was wrong of him—"

But the girl had turned discreetly away. "Sorry I

brought the matter up," she murmured. "I didn't mean to upset you."

"I'm not upset." But she was. She had to get away and gather herself together. The arrival of Stephen and this awful girl assistant had shaken her badly. She opened the door of the tiny room near the kitchen that she had allotted to herself, flopped down on the bed, clenched her teeth, and covered her face with her hands. "Blast! Oh, blast!"

"Blast who? Or what?" a familiar voice asked mildly, and she leaped to her feet. "It's advisable, if you don't want to be overheard indulging in an emotional storm, to shut the door behind you," said Louis, coming right into her room and shutting the door himself. "Is there anything I can do to help?"

"Yes," Rosalie stormed, flinging herself upright, her cheeks scarlet, "you can get another girl to help me and either send your lover packing or turn her into a guest. If you think I'm going to do everything for eighteen people while she swans around in six-inch heels . . ."

"Come, come," said Louis mildly. "She's not my lover."

"It's pretty clear she soon will be. I suppose she speaks Greek." Rosalie's mouth twisted with bitter sarcasm.

"As a matter of fact, she does."

Rosalie stared at him in open disbelief.

"That's why I gave her the job," Louis told her, his eyes glinting. "I've hit the jackpot, haven't I, with two girls who have both brains and beauty?" He came closer, only a step because the room was tiny, and stood looking down at her, his eyes veiled. "And since we're talking of importing lovers, may I suggest that what's good for the goose is good for the gander? Why didn't you tell me about Mr. Stephen Barrington?"

"Because I didn't know," she flared back.

"Oh, but you did," he retorted softly. "You were clearly expecting him. I'm not insensitive, you know. I've seldom seen such a picture of guilt and apprehension as I saw on your face as you stood waiting for us. Now, I'm not saying it's against the rules. But I'd just as soon remind you now as later on when the damage may be done that you're paid for being here, and he's paying." His voice hardened and there was a warning in it. "Let's not have any misunderstandings about that. When I said you were on duty twenty-four hours a day I meant it. You're in charge here, and I'm warning you. Twenty-four hours a day, seven days a week," he said, his eyes boring into her.

"You didn't tell me that," she flared at him. "Nobody works twenty-four hours a day, seven days a week."

"Was there any mention of a day off when we made the contract?" he inquired silkily. He had mentioned a day off when they talked in Athens. But also that she might entertain the guests then, she recalled.

"What contract? I signed no contract," she denied with heat, realizing she had been caught on the subject of the day off.

"Our verbal contract. I don't deal with the kind of people who need a signature under a list of rules," he told her scathingly.

"I know," she flashed at him. "You use them while they're following your rules, then throw them out when things go wrong."

He stared at her, his eyes narrowed, his face becoming grim. He moved right up to her so that his hot breath was on her face. "What made you say that?" he asked. His hands moved to her bare upper arms. The fingers tightened on her flesh.

"You got a girl pregnant and threw her out."

Breathless with shock at her outburst, Rosalie could only stare at him. She hadn't meant to say it. Not yet. Not until she had found a way to exact her revenge.

He did not reply, but the grip on her arms relaxed. She saw his eyes cloud over and without moving he seemed to recede from her. "I see," he said quietly. "You knew her? Fay Oliver? It is Fay Oliver you're talking about, I presume." His voice had a strange quality that she had not heard before.

Rosalie sat in dumb horror at the mess she had made of things. What on earth had induced her to say that? But she knew. She had an overwhelming urge, totally beyond her control, to hurt him; to embarrass him; to shame him. An emotion, she knew to her chagrin, that was connected with his hiring of the girl Janine.

"You were fond of her?" Louis asked, still in that strange voice. Again she nodded, unable to speak. He stood still for a moment as though perplexed, one hand to his brow; then quietly he turned and left the room.

Chapter Seven

That evening was all rush and scatter. Luckily, Rosalie had no more time to think about her personal problems. "Consider my position," she explained distractedly to Stephen when he protested that she had scarcely spoken to him. "There are eighteen people here—nineteen," she added with a bitter glance across at Janine seated on a low stone wall that divided the terrace from the rocky garden, casually examining her beautiful nails, ignoring the thin cats gathered about her. "All these people have dropped in from outer space and haven't got their bearings. I'm responsible for providing them with directions, information, advice . . . and I'm cook, handyman, and guide as well. You must understand that I'm not in a position to have a personal friend."

Stephen shrugged. "It'll settle down," he said.

"Why don't you go into the town, have a look around and get your bearings? Take some of the guests with you. There are tavernas on the quay where you can sample the ouzo. It's everybody's tipple." She told him about the colorful fishermen with their caïques, and the amusing, high-stepping pelicans. "In fact," she added, picking up a sheet of paper from a small pile, "I've made a map of the town to show you where Spiro's restaurant is, so if you like we could all meet there at eight or eight-thirty and have dinner together." Some of the guests had gathered around. They nodded in agreement.

"Where are the shops?" inquired the new assistant, looking up from the scrutiny of her nails. "I'd like to buy myself one of those lacy wool shawls."

Rosalie regarded her with level eyes, though she was seething inside. "I think you'll find plenty of time to choose a shawl to take home," she said. "You're not going to need it here. The evenings are really quite hot. I was about to start showing you the ropes. Mr. Alexander and I have drawn up a set of do's and don't's that you must know about for the benefit of the guests."

"Louis and I—we are on Christian-name terms, you know," the other girl said patronizingly, tossing her heavy black satin hair as she raised her exquisite face to meet Rosalie's, "have had our heads together for some hours. I can't imagine what you could tell me that he hasn't already dealt with. And since he is my employer"—she moved languidly upright, standing with one long leg bent, one hand on a hip, a model's elegant pose—"I think I'll take orders from him, thank you very much."

Biting her lip, Rosalie turned away. The group led by Stephen had already gone off down the hill chattering happily. Other guests came from the lower villas, fortunately diverting Rosalie with questions and small requests.

"I've made up an itinerary which is subject to popular vote," she said. "Of course you're free to do exactly as you like. The time and place of meals are the only static items, and even those of course you're free to miss or make your own arrangements about, on the understanding that you pay for yourselves. But there's a beautiful beach on the other side of the island, and we thought you might like to spend the first day there to get your suntans going."

"Lovely. That's what I need. A suntan," said Nan.

"I believe it's a nudist beach," said Janine, smoothing one hand suggestively down her beautifully slim hips. "That might be rather interesting."

Ignoring her, Rosalie turned back to the other girl. "There's a seafood restaurant, so you can stay all day at the beach. I've arranged a set menu."

"Super."

"And the next day we plan to visit the island of Delos, about twenty minutes in a caïque, if you all agree. It's historically significant, so I daresay most of you will know something about it."

"And what you don't know, Rosalie will fill in," a familiar voice said behind her. "She's a mine of information." Rosalie swung around, her eyes sparking, but Louis' expression could not have been more bland. She busied herself handing out the maps she had made, and the last of the guests departed.

Janine looked up at Louis from under her long lashes. "I've been told I can't go down to the town and buy myself a shawl," she said, pouting.

"Quite right," Louis replied lightly. "You don't need a shawl. Now, there's a lot for you two to discuss." He addressed the new assistant. "Has Rosalie shown you the ropes?"

She smiled in that feline way she had. "I'd rather take orders from you," she said sweetly.

108

"There won't be any orders," Louis replied, still in that bland, detached manner. "You girls will be working together. But first of all Rosalie will fill you in, since she's the one who has made all the arrangements."

"Forgive me," murmured the new girl. "I had the impression she was to be the boss."

"I'm the boss." The cryptic statement was softened by a smile.

Rosalie was seething. Louis was being treacherous. Had he not told her she was to be in charge, and this girl her assistant? Now they had met and she knew the type of person Janine was, she was certain things would work no other way.

"Are you staying for the whole two weeks?" Janine asked, fluttering her long lashes at Louis.

"It depends on how things go in London. I'll certainly be here for a few days. Now . . ." He picked up a little red table and set three green chairs around it. "Let's sit down and get to work."

None of the guests returned. By seven-thirty Janine had, or Rosalie assumed she had, a working knowledge of what was going on, but she was frankly worried about many aspects of the other girl. Her long painted fingernails, her indolent air. Her totally unsuitable clothes. She was angry with Louis for taking on such a girl on the pretext that she spoke Greek. It was only necessary that one of them speak the language, and Rosalie could do that. "Come on now," said Louis, rising from his chair. "Let's go down to the port and I'll buy you two an apéritif."

Janine went to her room. Ten minutes later she returned in a sleek jump suit, as black as her lustrous hair and with a plunging neckline that left nothing to the imagination. She had changed into a pair of strappy black sandals with extremely high heels. "Very elegant," Louis commented appreciatively.

"You risk breaking your ankle in those shoes," said Rosalie, trying desperately to sound cool but with anger and apprehension showing through.

"Then Louis will have to carry me home," simpered the new girl.

"Aren't you going to change?" Louis asked. He looked pointedly at Rosalie's jeans.

"I don't think I could compete," she murmured, glancing away as she picked up her shoulder bag from the back of a chair and started across the terrace, chin high.

"You're too modest."

He looked very much at home walking between the two of them, Rosalie thought sardonically as they went down the steep incline into the back of the town. With a pang she remembered Fay, wondering if some other girl had walked in just like this and tempted him away just when Fay was expecting to marry him. Thank goodness, she thought fiercely, she was not vulnerable. There had been that bad moment when they were fleeing the nightclub, but it was not going to happen again.

They walked along the quay and joined a group of their guests outside a taverna. They had made friends with a pelican and were feeding it tidbits from their table. Hurriedly, Stephen picked up a spare chair, and Rosalie realized uncomfortably that she would have to sit beside him. Janine had slid her arm through Louis' and was waiting with the calm, expectant air of one who anticipates that people will rush to attend to her needs. The guests scattered apart good-naturedly, adjusting the seating to accommodate the three newcomers.

"I'm glad you got away," Stephen said happily,

resting one arm across the back of Rosalie's chair, his pleasant face beneath its thatch of fair hair warm with welcome. "What a lovely evening!"

"Every evening in Mykonos is lovely," Louis told him with confidence. "It won't rain until October or November. One thing you don't have to do out here is worry about the weather. Keep an eye on the sun, though. We don't want a case of sunstroke."

"You've got a hat?" Stephen asked, concernedly, and Rosalie flushed with annoyance at his assumption of the role of loving guardian.

"You forget," she said crisply, "that I am very much at home in this part of the world."

"Ouzo?" asked Louis, but before she could as much as nod Stephen had butted in.

"I'll get Rosalie's drink."

Rosalie squirmed in her seat. "I'd rather not, thank you. I'll have a Coke." This was intolerable. She would have to take Stephen aside and make it clear to him that there was to be no going back to the days before Fay had come between them.

Louis caught the waiter's eye. "Two ouzos here and one over there," he said imperturbably. Rosalie tried hard not to react at the high-handed way in which he had ignored her request for a Coke. Louis lit two cigarettes and gave one to Janine, the gesture as casual as though he had known her a long time and was in tune with her needs. Or else, Rosalie thought with an inexplicable sinking feeling inside, they had found themselves in perfect harmony on meeting, as one occasionally does with a stranger.

The drinks came. Louis tossed some notes carelessly onto the tray. As Stephen began to protest he said curtly, "Don't worry, Barrington, I'll have one on you later." Stephen looked put out but said nothing, and unexpectedly Rosalie felt sorry for him.

Later, as they straggled up the narrow, brightly lit, colorful streets toward Spiro's restaurant, she found herself side by side with Stephen. "I'm most dreadfully sorry about what happened," she said. "You know that. We talked about it before. But there's no going back. I thought you understood. Surely you want to be clear of—of—the whole sad business."

He looked into her face, his own serious, "I'm sorry, too," he said. "I'm sorry for what I did to you. Letting you down like that. I want to make it up to you." He squeezed her arm.

"You can't," she told him bleakly. And then, with irritation: "I've said there's no going back." She tried to shrug her arm out of his grip.

"Did I hurt you so much? Of course—"

She broke in, her voice unintentionally sharp because she was embarrassed, because she did not want to hurt him. "It was over between us long ago," she said. "Please, please, let it stay dead." She saw the distress in his face and was immediately sorry she had spoken that way. She reached for his hand and squeezed it. "I feel guilty about what Fay did to you," she whispered. "But it's not up to me to make amends. Truly it isn't. You wouldn't want a relationship based on guilt, would you?" He slipped an arm around her waist. "Guilt on both sides," she added hurriedly, trying to slide away from him and not succeeding. "You feel guilty about leaving me for Fay. And I'm guilty on her behalf, for the way she made use of you."

"We're going to pretend it never happened," Stephen said confidently and to her chagrin leaned down to kiss her on the cheek.

She sensed eyes on her, boring into her. She looked up, her face aflame. Louis was coming up beside her, walking with Janine, her arm linked with his. Their eyes met. His were unreadable, shadowed as he stood with his back to a streetlamp. "Let's leave the lovers in peace," said Janine. "Come on, Louis. I'm starving." And then they were gone, striding ahead into the shadows.

Rosalie said bleakly, "Louis has made it quite clear that he expects me to give of my best. You must have realized how pointed that was. You heard him say 'twenty-four hours a day.'"

"Nobody works twenty-four hours a day," Stephen asserted stoutly. "I'll speak to him."

Rosalie felt an uprush of anger at his interference, but she kept her voice calm. "No, Stephen, you will not."

"But of course I will," he protested. "You clearly need someone to stand up for you."

She wriggled away from him. "I don't want to be unkind. It's the last thing I wish to be after what you've been through, but I must say this. You came here without my knowledge. I'd have stopped you if I could." She saw the disappointment in his face, and her heart went out to him. "I'm sorry."

"You're bitter," he said, "Heaven knows. I had nothing out of it. I got my comeuppance. Please, Rosalie, let bygones be bygones and start again." The crowds were swirling around them, jostling them as they passed in the narrow cobblestoned street.

"We can't discuss it here," Rosalie told him despairingly.

Stephen was silent momentarily; then he said gently, infuriatingly, "I'll win you around."

Something like fear came up in her. A knowledge that she was not going to be able to cope with the sudden complications of her life. Yet she had to try. She had never known Stephen to be deliberately cruel. She had to take a chance with him. "I want you

113

to promise not to mention our—our—anything about our association. I mean about Fay," she corrected herself hurriedly, "to anyone here."

A sharp glint came into his eyes. "And particularly to Alexander? It's obvious he's making a play for the new girl, but something was going on between you before she arrived, wasn't it? One can't help noticing. He's taunting you, isn't he? He doesn't quite look in your direction when he touches her, but one has a feeling . . ." His gray eyes were all at once not quite so kind.

"Nothing has been going on between us," Rosalie retorted icily. "Janine is a very beautiful girl. Any man would be attracted to her."

"Come," he said brusquely. "We'd better push on. We're miles behind the others. It's too late for secrets, anyway. I told the girl I was sitting with on the plane that we were friends. And anyway, it's obvious."

Indeed it was, she thought angrily. "You had no right to say we were engaged," she told him, "because we never were."

"Almost," he retorted stubbornly. "Almost engaged. And we would have been married if that little—"

"I will not discuss Fay," she burst out, silencing him. "We both loved her and she must rest in peace." They were coming around the corner into the square and Spiro's restaurant was in view. Their party was already seated at the little square tables under the bright bougainvillea. It had been one of Rosalie's stipulations, and Spiro had graciously agreed, that Louis' guests should have tables in the open air. Rosalie looked around for a vacant seat.

"There's a table for two," Louis said silkily. "We saved it especially for you." He indicated a tiny one discreetly placed beneath a cascade of blossom directly on his right, not an arm's length away, where, for all the romance of its situation, he would be able to overhear every word they spoke. With a sinking heart Rosalie thanked him and with all eyes on herself and Stephen they made their way toward it.

Next morning Rosalie wakened early, coming slowly to consciousness with the knowledge that something was wrong. She opened her eyes and looked around the bare little room. Time to get up and face the day with all its complications. She hauled herself out of bed, donned jeans, T-shirt, and sandals, brushed her hair until it shone, then fixed it into a knot on the crown of her head. Looking critically in the narrow mirror on the wall, she thought she looked neat and workmanlike. The lacquer had chipped off her toenails. She took a bottle of remover from a drawer and wiped the remainder away, but she did not have the heart to replace it.

From the locked drawer in the kitchen she helped herself to a fold of notes, carefully locked it again and pocketed the key, took the big basket she had purchased at a market stall from under the table, then set off down the hill. At this hour of the morning the streets were already alive with locals hurrying about their business. Workmen carrying forks and shovels were making their way inland to attend to their vegetable patches before the heat of the day was upon them. A tiny donkey with a load of hay as tall as itself plodded patiently along, led by an old woman in black widow's weeds. A vegetable cart rattled down the slope toward the market.

Even before Rosalie came to the street where the bakery lay, the smell of newly made bread assailed her nostrils. She lifted her head and sniffed appreciatively. Stavros the baker, a solid, dark little chunk of a man, greeted her with enthusiasm. "It is the beautiful Mees Rosalie," he cried, gesticulating in the Greek way. She answered him in Greek, but he replied insistently in his broken English. There were not many occasions on which Rosalie needed to speak Greek, but command of the language was a considerable asset nonetheless. The locals who dealt with tourists spoke limited English, but it would not have been easy to do business with the builders, the furniture makers, and the plumbers if she had not been able to speak to them in Greek. "I haf your rolls all ready and only just out of the oven. Special for you," Stavros added winningly, taking her basket and leading her behind the counter into the kitchen where rows of loaves of all shapes and sizes were lined up and the air was heavy with the delicious aroma of them. He tossed the pile carelessly into the basket, chattering happily in his broken English all the while. "There, Mees Rosalie," he said as he handed it back to her. "Such beeg load you have to carry! Your employer must buy you donkey."

"How lovely!" she exclaimed delightedly. "I must suggest it to him."

"And now I will be sad until tomorrow, until you come again." She laughed happily, feeling her spirits lift. How I love Greece, she said to herself as she went back up the hill with a lighter heart. She was continually warmed by the friendliness and charm of the people.

But her spirits plummeted to rock bottom as she entered the kitchen. Janine, a vision in a bright pink blouse with plunging neckline and tight trousers, was sitting on one of the stools Rosalie had painted, leaning an elbow on the table, her palm supporting her forehead, her beautiful eyes closed, the long

116

lashes dark on pale cheeks. "What on earth is the matter?"

Janine opened her beautiful eyes, looking pathetically at the other girl. "The matter is that Louis introduced me to the local brandy. Oh, what a head I have got!"

"You'd better go back to bed," said Rosalie bleakly, her heart sinking at the thought of producing breakfast for twenty on her own.

"I can't," wailed Janine. "It was Louis who hauled me out. He made me get up. He was so callous. He laughed."

"Then you had better put your best foot forward," Rosalie told her, not without sympathy, though she found herself holding back a smile. "If I were you I'd start by getting into more suitable gear," she observed tartly. "Splashes of dishwater won't improve those expensive-looking pants. Didn't you bring any jeans? Or shorts?" she added, thinking of the diversion Janine would cause in the kind of shorts Rosalie could imagine her wearing.

"I did," returned Janine, looking pathetic, "but really, I felt so bad I couldn't take an interest in what I was putting on."

Rosalie crushed the cynical comment that rose to her lips. "I'll make you a strong cup of coffee. But in the meantime, I think you should get into suitable gear. There's not much time to spare."

"Nobody's up yet," the other girl muttered plaintively.

"The rules are that breakfast is to be ready for any guest at any time after seven o'clock," Rosalie said lightly.

"Whose rules? Who made them?" Janine came sufficiently alive to look resentful and suspicious.

"I did."

Janine rose, elegant and beautiful with her dark hair massed around her shoulders. "I take orders from Louis," she said sullenly.

"As a matter of fact, I think you'll find that my rules hold," Rosalie told her crisply, "but do check with Louis. It's better that you should be satisfied in your own mind." She picked up the percolator and carried it to the sink. "And by the way, bare feet won't work any more than those excessively high heels you wore last night," she said, looking down critically at the girl's slender, pretty bare feet with their beautifully manicured nails. "If you haven't any canvas shoes or sandals I'd suggest you run down at the first opportunity and buy some. I mean, after we've done the dishes. Those rough little plants that grow between the stones are pretty sharp, and some of them may be poisonous."

The other girl flounced out. At least I galvanized her into action, Rosalie thought, suppressing a bleak little smile as she put the coffee on to percolate. She tied a frilly apron she had bought in the market around her waist and took a duster out onto the terrace to wipe down the painted tables. Then she piled the big tray with plates, cups, knives, and all the paraphernalia of breakfast.

Louis appeared in the doorway. His dark hair fell across his forehead in a shining sweep, as though it had been tossed there carelessly by the wind. His torso was, as usual, bare where his shirt was unbuttoned to the waist, and there was such a virile, male air about him, like a young god with the world at his feet, that Rosalie drew back and her breath caught in her throat. She recovered herself quickly, saying crisply, "I don't think you've made it quite clear to my assistant that she *is* my assistant. Perhaps you'd like to attend to that when you have a spare moment. And you might have a serious word with her about clothes and work. The plunging neckline may be her fault, but I should think the hangover is yours."

Louis chuckled. "In her state she probably reached blindly for the nearest garment."

"As she said. And the nearest garment just happened to be the sexiest bit of gear she had," Rosalie rejoined bleakly, avoiding his eyes. "You really have done me a great disservice in bringing that girl here. She's going to be absolutely hopeless. And if she speaks Greek I'll eat my hat. Maybe she has fooled you, but, as you know, Greek is a very difficult language. It's not the sort of thing any fool can pick up in five minutes."

"You've a sharp tongue in your head," Louis commented, but he said it detachedly, as though he were thinking of something else, and his eyes danced with amusement.

Something about his manner inflamed Rosalie. "You could have had an affair with her without bringing her to Mykonos," she spat at him. Louis came right into the kitchen, carefully closing the door behind him.

"What a little spitfire you can be when roused," he marveled, resting his hands on her shoulders and looking searchingly into her face. She tried to shrug his hands away, but his fingers gripped more tightly. "Some girls," he said softly, "need a provocative neckline to prove something about themselves. There are others who scream their sexuality in working gear. What, if I may ask a pertinent question, do you imagine that rather tight little T-shirt does to a man?" Tight! Blushing scarlet, Rosalie glanced down in alarm at her small, firm breasts where they jutted against the thin material. The shirt was indeed old.

She had not realized how much it had shrunk. "You don't have to flaunt yourself here, you know," Louis went on tauntingly. "The Greek male is nothing if not vulnerable. He'd follow a veiled and robed Muslim lady with hope in his heart."

"How dare you!" She struggled to raise her right hand.

"Hit me, would you? I'd advise against that. You might find you've started something you can't stop."

"Let me go," she seethed.

"Not until you've calmed down. It's well known some women get their kicks from violence," he taunted her again.

"How dare you!" He did let her go then.

"Well," he drawled, "you do react rather well—I mean rather satisfactorily when the going is, shall I say, robust?" And then, with one of his quick changes of mood, he added, "It's time the tables were ready. Let me carry this tray out for you. I hear a noise like the sound of a rising tourist."

Chapter Eight

As she sped among the tables putting out plates and
cutlery Rosalie tried to put Louis and his alarming
behavior out of her mind; tried not to see his tall
figure hovering; tried to calm her inflamed senses;
told herself firmly not to be disturbed by him. He was
only her employer, after all. She should never have
started calling him Louis. Never allowed him to use
her Christian name. She heaved an enormous sigh. It
would not have been possible, of course. Everyone
used Christian names these days. She put out of her
mind the fact that she had let her feelings run away
with her so that now he knew she was connected with
Fay. Heaven only knew what he was assuming from
her presence here. She could not think about it now.

It was delightful on the big terrace at this hour with
the sun, still not very high in the east, silvering the bay
far below. The guests straggled out of bed in twos and

threes. They seated themselves at the small tables on the vine-hung terrace. Louis went off into the town on a mission of his own. Janine took her time about changing. Rosalie had all the tables set, the food out, and the coffee ready before she appeared.

But to Rosalie's relief the new girl now wore jeans and a loose blouse. The jeans looked as though they had been shrunk onto her, but the blouse gave her a faint aura of respectability. She now wore flat-heeled sandals, Rosalie noted with relief. She had no desire to be ministering to a broken ankle. She smiled her approval, but Janine did not respond. Rosalie, who had been flitting in and out of the tables pouring coffee and exchanging pleasantries with the guests, took time off to slip into the kitchen and get a cup for the new girl. "Sit down with the guests," she said kindly, "and have something to eat. I can manage now." The other girl muttered her thanks and went out to the terrace. Afterward, when the guests had gone off to catch the bus for the beach Janine rose.

"If I'm to be dogsbody, I'd better get on with it," she said resentfully and began to gather up dishes.

So Louis had spoken to her! Rosalie flashed her a cheerful smile. "You're not a dogsbody," she assured the new girl. "We'll share the work. You mustn't mind my being in charge. Someone has to be responsible. But we'll share the nicer jobs. I do hope you can cook." Janine nodded. "We'll do that together, then. And the marketing. It's quite a big job, but it's fun."

"Don't tell me we have to carry food for all these people up that terrible hill."

Rosalie kept her expression determinedly cheerful. "It's not such a terrible hill when you're wearing sensible shoes. And when you look at the view you must be glad to be here," she added encouragingly. "Down in the town it's very hot and shut in. You must have noticed last night that the lanes between the houses are very narrow. It becomes oppressive. Here, we get a lovely breeze every afternoon." She was piling the dishes as she chatted, concentrating on her work. She jumped when Janine said, "Here's your boyfriend."

Turning, she saw Stephen coming back along the path from the road. Her heart sank. "I thought I'd give you a hand," he said. "Then perhaps you could come to the beach, too."

It was all Rosalie could do to keep the exasperation out of her voice. "You must accept the fact that I'm here to work, Stephen, and you are a paying guest."

"That doesn't mean I can't help you," he said stubbornly, putting his towel and swimming trunks down on a chair and preparing to take the tray from her.

"What a nice boyfriend!" exclaimed Janine, looking at Rosalie with a gleam of malice in her eyes. "Of course you must stay and help us, Stephen. Why not?"

"There's no question of my going to Platiyalos today," Rosalie told him steadily. "There's marketing to be done."

"I'll help you with that."

"And I have to oversee the two women who are coming to clean and tidy the villas. This is their first day."

"I could do that," offered Janine.

Rosalie bit back a retort that she was sure overseeing staff would suit Janine very well. She said instead, "I'm sorry. I'm in charge. If you wouldn't mind starting on the dishes, Janine, I'd be grateful, though how you're going to manage with those fingernails I really don't know."

"I'll wash," offered Stephen, jumping at the opportunity of wedging himself in. He picked up the tray and hurried into the kitchen. Janine, with a triumphant look, took a bundle of knives and went after him. There was nothing to do but join them. When Rosalie entered the kitchen Stephen already had his hands in a sinkful of soapy water and Janine was standing beside him with a tea towel in her hands. Rosalie took another one.

"Quite the domestic little scene," a dry voice said from the doorway, and Rosalie jumped guiltily, swinging around to see Louis leaning laconically against the doorpost.

Janine said, bright-faced, innocent, and treacherous, "He can't bear to go to the beach without Rosalie." She sidled up to Louis, fluttering her lashes as Rosalie stood dumbly by, a prey to inarticulate fury. "You'll let her off to have a swim with Stephen, won't you?"

Louis said coldly and uncompromisingly, "Barrington, if you want to make yourself useful that's your business, but I employ these girls and they know the terms of their employment. Swimming is not on their agenda today."

Consumed with embarrassment, Rosalie knew that no protest of hers was going to help. Stephen meant well. She went on wiping the dishes in silent humiliation. Louis said, addressing her directly, "The two housemaids are here. You'd better come and talk to them, Rosalie." His eyes were cold on her. Then suddenly he smiled. "You didn't tell me they go by the delightful names of Cleopatra and Helena."

She followed him out. "I haven't had much of an opportunity to tell you anything," she retorted aloofly, still smarting under his earlier rebuke. She greeted the women and proceeded to direct them to the work she had outlined when she engaged them.

Louis disappeared. Stephen was quietly insistent about accompanying the girls to the market. Short of insulting him, Rosalie could see no way of dissuading him. And he was remarkably useful, she had to admit, good-naturedly carrying the heavy baskets. They were back at the villa early, Rosalie found herself admitting grudgingly, because of Stephen's help. "I'm sorry we can't have lunch with you, Stephen," she told him apologetically, "but your lunch has been ordered at the fish café on the beach. Janine and I haven't time to go over there."

Irrepressibly he replied, his face shining with good-will, "Then I'll eat with you, and pay for myself."

If she did not feel so guilty about him, Rosalie thought, biting her lip, she could tell him brusquely to make himself scarce. As it was, she compromised. "Janine and I have a great deal to do this afternoon and we don't want to be diverted. Preparation of dinner for this crowd is no light task. So if you don't mind, Stephen, we'd be grateful if you'd leave us on our own." He looked crestfallen, but he went, reluctantly, and Rosalie heaved a sigh of relief.

"You could have retained him to peel the potatoes," Janine said resentfully as Stephen went off disconsolately to catch the bus.

"We'll manage," Rosalie told her briskly.

The two girls worked hard to produce a meal that was a combination of Greek and English cooking. They peeled a mountain of vegetables. Louis had thoughtfully provided them with a blender. Using one of the big potbellied urns Rosalie had bought locally, they made a delicious vegetable soup. Then they made a lamb stew with the lovely fat purple eggplants, green and red peppers, almonds, and—"for the gastronomically unadventurous," Rosalie said, smiling— "a lot of potatoes." Louis had brought an enormous

125

Cheddar cheese out from England. "Everyone doesn't take to sheep's milk cheese," he had commented as he handed it over. And there were enormous tins of crackers in the store cupboard. Luckily, big purple figs were in season for dessert. Otherwise, fruit wasn't so easy to come by.

"I'd like to make some honey cakes," Rosalie remarked, flipping through the Greek recipe book Louis had provided. Janine heaved an exhausted sigh.

"Really! Who are you trying to impress?" she asked querulously. "They can have honey cakes every time they eat out. Don't you really think we've done enough for one day?" She looked in disgust at her stained fingers. "And I've broken two of my nails."

Rosalie found herself looking at the other girl with compassion. "Perhaps you didn't realize what you were coming to," she offered. "Why did you take the job?"

"Probably for the same reason you did," she retorted snappily. "Louis Alexander is a very attractive man."

"He is also a very callous one," said Rosalie, wondering even as she said it why she should bother to warn this girl who was undoubtedly an opportunist and possibly a gold digger into the bargain.

The pretty features tightened into a feline smile. "I quite understand you would want to warn me off," she retorted. "Don't think I didn't see the shock on your face when I arrived. Since we're exchanging confidences, what's your little game, anyway? Did you intend to play one man off against the other?"

Rosalie undid her apron. "I think we're both tired," she said, assuming a brisk, no-nonsense voice, though she was seething inside. "I suggest you have a siesta. Or else, if you'd like to catch a bus over to the beach and come back with the others I shan't mind.

We're not likely to eat before eight o'clock or nine and everything's under way."

The other girl's face lit up briefly; then suspicion showed in the beautiful eyes. "You want to get me into trouble?"

"Of course I don't. I'll take full responsibility. In fact, I'm going to have a swim myself at the little pebble beach below the windmill. It's not very special, but I can be down there and back in twenty minutes, which is all the time I can spare if I'm to make the honey cakes."

Janine's face was full of longing. "And if Louis is at Platiyalos?"

"It will be nice for you. Just tell him I sent you," Rosalie suggested sweetly. "And while you're away I suggest you file those nails down," she added, softening the request with a laugh. "I don't think the guests would be very amused to find one of them in the soup."

Janine tossed her beautiful head. "I can't make out whether you're sincere or just very clever. I wouldn't be surprised, in fact, if Louis was down at that pebble beach of yours."

"You and I have to work together," Rosalie said wearily. "Life will be a great deal easier for us both if we're friends. When I told you Louis was callous I did it with the best of intentions. I wouldn't like to see you hurt. I mean that."

"Thanks." But Janine said it sneeringly, tossing her head. "I'm off to Platiyalos."

Rosalie turned the gas down low under the two enormous pots, slipped into a bikini and canvas shoes, and hurried up over the brow of the hill. Two black-robed priests and a nun passed her, walking slowly beneath the hot sun. She found the steep little path bordered by late primroses, rich purple iris, and the lovely campanula with its blue tubular flowers. The sweet scents assailed her nostrils as she ran. Somehow, in the clear air of Greece she was always more conscious of flower scents. They seemed suspended everywhere on the air. She skipped from bend to bend, taking the steps two at a time, her hair flying loose now that she had released it from its restraining band. The sea looked wonderful, rippling gently in the breeze that always came up after midday. She ran down the narrow track between some white-painted villas, turned a corner, and ran slap into Louis.

"Well!" he exclaimed putting out his arms to steady her. "What's the hurry? The sea won't go away."

She laughed breathlessly as she extricated herself. "I didn't want to leave the meal for too long."

"If you go back up at that rate you'll have a heart attack for sure." Then, turning, he said, "Come on, then. I'll join you. I've just sneaked a swim myself."

She saw then that his thick black hair was dripping and myriads of water droplets glistened on his sun-tanned shoulders. She felt her heart give a great treacherous surge of pleasure. "Race you."

They were away, sprinting down the narrow path, leaping over a low wall of rock onto the pebbles and then the sand. Rosalie flung her towel down where Louis had already dropped his and dashed after him, running and laughing as the water slowed her impetus until she lost her balance and began to swim. It was wonderful, after the hard work of the day and the heat of the kitchen, to feel the cool, clean water on her skin. Rosalie had a new sense of exhilaration that sent her spirits flying high. Difficulties drifted from her mind. She turned over on her back to float. When a firm hand on her shoulder sent her underwater she drifted down willingly, her hair tangling around her head in silken strands.

Time swept by as they swam, floated, and cavorted like dolphins, sensuously relishing every moment. Her treacherous mind told her the dinner would come to no harm. After all, what could happen, except that the gas might go out? And that was unlikely. And who needed honey cakes? There were plenty of figs. It had only been a thought.

An arm came around her neck. She brought herself upright with a gasp. "Have you ever been kissed underwater?" asked a teasing voice, and suddenly she was sinking, clamped in Louis' strong arms. She felt his lips on hers and a wild, exultant cry fled through her. They drifted to the surface still locked together. As they broke the surface both burst out laughing. She wanted to be angry with him, knew she should be. After all, he had probably been kissing Janine last night. Maybe he had even slept with her? But this was only horseplay, she told herself. It didn't mean a thing. Greece always did this to her—sent her spirits flying like wild birds. Made her forget everything but the moment.

At last, regretfully, she struggled ashore feeling renewed, invigorated, and ready for the rest of the day's work. "That was lovely," she said as they toweled themselves dry. "How did you come to be here?"

"I had to break into Nicholas' siesta—he lives just over there," explained Louis, pointing to a modest little dwelling painted pink and snuggling up against the silver-gray trunk of an enormous eucalyptus tree. "I wanted to inspect his caïque for the trip to Delos tomorrow and make certain he had everything ship-shape." He added apologetically, "I know you've got it all fixed, but the safety of the guests is ultimately my responsibility. So, as I had to pass by the beach, I made certain I just happened to have swimming trunks under my shorts. It's a lovely life, Rosalie, isn't it?"

She nodded.

"I was captivated by Greece the first time I set eyes on it. I'm only sorry I have to go," he went on regretfully as they started back up the path. She felt a sudden pang, a sense of approaching loss.

"When do you go?"

"As soon as I'm quite certain the setup is working and everyone's happy. Of course I should stay for the first full package of two weeks, then leave it to you, but"—he gave her a quizzical look—"I've a feeling you're going to cope very well. I might give it another three days."

"Janine will be disappointed." She couldn't imagine why she had said that. She could have bitten her tongue out afterward.

He gave her an odd look but did not reply.

"What time is Nicholas coming around with the caïque in the morning?" she asked brightly, trying to pretend to herself that that silly slip of the tongue had not occurred.

"About ten-thirty. Can you make it by then?"

"Why not? It's a very simple lunch I've planned. Rolls and cold meats and hard-boiled eggs. I'll wash the salad stuff tonight and have it all ready in the fridge. And Spiro has promised that one of his men will deliver a dozen bottles of wine to the caïque."

"Great," Louis approved.

They had started to climb the steep hill. Wild roses were burgeoning everywhere out of the dry, rocky soil, their scent heavy on the air. "You're coming, then?"

"Of course. To drink wine on the summit of Mount Cynthus where the great god Zeus crouched watching Leto give birth to Apollo. What more could a man ask

130

of tomorrow?" Momentarily, her heart seemed to fly on silver wings, and then she remembered Fay. Some part of her deep down inside hardened and went cold. But it did not last. Her spirits were too high. They refused to be put down.

They came up over the top of the hill puffing, their faces flushed from the exertion, and raced across the stony ground where wild flowers grew, pausing only when they reached the terrace of the villa.

"Hello," said a bleak voice. "I thought you didn't have time for a swim." Rosalie looked up into Stephen's hostile eyes. She crushed back the feeling of guilt that was always near the surface when Stephen was around and said lightly, "I had twenty minutes to spare, so I shot down to the bay."

"And Alexander just happened to be there," Stephen retorted sarcastically. "I happen to have been here nearly an hour. If that's your idea of twenty minutes—"

He broke off as Louis cut in equably. "What's time? It's all in the mind. You're on holiday, Barrington. Throw your watch away and enjoy yourself."

He tossed the words over his shoulder as he strolled casually down the little stepped path to the villa where he slept.

"If I'd known there was something going on between you two I wouldn't have come," Stephen said sourly. Rosalie looked at him with the compassion that always welled up when she had to remember what Fay had done to him.

"I didn't ask you to come, Stephen," she said gently. "I'm very sorry if I gave the impression at any time that there could be anything between us. And just to clear up any misunderstanding, there is nothing, absolutely nothing, between Louis and me. In fact, I despise him. He's ruthless and callous. I wouldn't dream of getting on any other terms with him but employer/employee. And Louis *did* happen to be on the beach when I slipped down for a quick swim. He was on business, but he had his swimming trunks on under his jeans. That's why the twenty minutes stretched out." She smiled. "When the boss says don't hurry back, one doesn't." She was standing before him on the vine-shaded veranda, slender and trim in her bright gold bikini that set off her suntan to perfection. "I don't know why I should bother to explain this to you," she went on. But you could not tell a man you were sorry for him. She heaved an enormous sigh. Perhaps when she had found a way to pay Louis back the guilt she felt toward Stephen would lessen.

Stephen's eyes brightened. "I'll win you around," he said warmly. He stood facing her. "You're so lovely, Rosalie. You're worth two of Fay."

Rosalie said bleakly, "I don't want to talk about Fay, Stephen. Now or ever. I thought I had made that clear to you. What's done is done and was buried with her. She was my sister and—"

"She wasn't your sister. Not even your half sister," interposed Stephen, his voice suddenly hot with denial, "and I'm bound to tell you—"

"You're bound to tell me nothing," Rosalie retorted sharply, swinging around on her heel. "I'm going to change. I've work to do." But he hurried after her, right to the door of her room. "You're holding it against me that I let you down," he protested. "I want to tell you how bitterly I regretted that. If only we could go back to the way it was before Fay turned up. If I could only make you understand what power that girl had over a man . . ."

"I know," Rosalie said gently. "She was lovely and she had something irresistible. We all adored her."

With a rush of contrition she kissed Stephen softly on the cheek and then shut the door gently in his face, leaving him standing there.

The guests straggled back from the beach sun-burned and happy, trailing sand into the villa, sloshing water all over the floor as they showered, apologizing laughingly, blaming the plumbing.

"What on earth have you done with Janine?" Rosalie asked as she skipped between the tables on the terrace in her fresh cotton dress and pretty apron, setting out glasses. The guests had bought their own apéritifs and the whole place was taking on the jolly atmosphere of a taverna.

At that moment Janine came wandering up the path, seductively attired in the briefest of tops and wearing a flimsy see-through skirt over bikini pants that were little more than a G-string.

"Oh, dear, I'm late," she said, pouting. "I really couldn't help it. The bus started without any warning, so I went back into the water to wait for the next one, and it didn't come for absolutely ages."

Stephen said, looking after Janine as she went off down the path to the lower villa, moving her elegant hips slinkily, "She's not going to be much help to you. What can I do?"

"You can sit down with the others and enjoy an apéritif," said Rosalie, adopting a brisk, impersonal voice. "Janine is being paid to work. I'm sure she will be back soon."

But when Janine returned half an hour later she was accompanied attentively by Louis. They looked magnificent together, Rosalie thought grudgingly, watching them as they approached the terrace. He was wearing one of his beautiful silk shirts, the rich cream color of it setting off his tan, the buttons as always undone to the waist. And tonight he wore finely

133

tailored jeans that clung to his neat hips with a perfection she had not seen on other men. His clothes had a casual, throwaway elegance that was difficult to pin down. They were not conspicuous, they merged with the more ordinary look of the clothes the guests wore, and yet one knew instinctively it cost the earth to produce that special note of distinction. Silence fell across the group on the terrace as the two approached. Janine was wearing a calf-length, fine cotton dress in deep violet, with stovepipe matching trousers. The outfit gave her an Indian look. To complete the picture her hair was twisted into a soft roll at the nape of her neck. A low gasp came from somewhere nearby. "Isn't she gorgeous! No wonder Louis is smitten."

Rosalie spun around, a scathing retort on her lips, but she bit it back in time. "Just the gear for dishing out dinner," she said lightly, forcing a stiff smile onto her face.

Surprisingly, Janine went to work without being asked, setting out plates and cutlery. "I couldn't help noticing the look on your face," she said to Rosalie when the two girls found themselves alone in the kitchen, "but I do assure you it's possible to be efficient as well as elegant." She cast a patronizing glance over Rosalie's unsophisticated attire. "There's no more reason why I should slop soup over this outfit than that you should slop it over that very 'suitable' dress of yours." As she spoke she grimaced at the apron Rosalie had bought in the market, started to put it on, then held it out at arm's length, looking at it critically. "Would you like to swap? Yours matches my outfit!" Rosalie was tempted to hurl a splintering reply, but she controlled her exasperation and obligingly undid the bow, handing the frilly apron to the other girl. "And anyway, Louis has offered to help with the dishes so that we can get away to see the Greek dancing. They're all going tonight, you know. I daresay Stephen will be taking you. Perhaps he'd like to help with the clearing up as well."

"If the guests had been expected to help it would have been mentioned in the brochure," Rosalie retorted and was immediately sorry for her churlishness when Janine returned, "You've been working too hard. In this hot climate, and with the late nights we keep, it's essential to have a siesta. You really ought. You were up early this morning, weren't you? It's too long a day."

Thrown by the sudden change to sympathy, Rosalie retorted, "You're going to have to be up early yourself tomorrow. I want you to come down to the bakery with me. There's extra to carry because of the packed lunch, and besides, I want to show you where the bakery is so that you can take your turn collecting bread in the mornings. Now, would you mind ladling the soup into the tureen, please."

Chapter Nine

Dinner was pronounced a great success. Louis, magnanimous and appreciative, called for a toast to the cooks. Everyone drank it willingly, in retsina. Afterward, there was a delightful surprise as guests rushed to help with the clearing up. "Why not?" queried Nan. "We've been lying on the beach all day. It will do us good."

"But this is our job," Rosalie protested.

"Forget it. Many hands make light work. Then we can all go off together to the dancing."

They hurried from table to table, good-naturedly bumping into each other, rushing the dishes to the kitchen, where Louis undid Rosalie's apron and donned it himself. Rosalie protested, but laughingly the others pushed her out and the place became a hive of activity. Someone turned on a radio and several couples started to dance.

After that it would have been churlish to go straight

to bed as Rosalie had intended. She mingled with the merry throng as they went off down the hill into the town.

Louis was out in front with the glamorous Janine. To Rosalie's chagrin, word had gone around that Stephen was here to patch up their broken engagement. People walking with her would quietly melt away into the crowd as he approached, leaving the two of them together. And by the same token it was assumed that Janine and Louis belonged together. Rosalie was chatting happily to the young man called Brian when Stephen came up on her free side. He took her arm in a proprietary manner. Brian saw and began to move away, but Rosalie shook her arm free and moved with the other man, endeavoring to keep the conversation going. Her heart sank when he remained silent, casting embarrassed glances in Stephen's direction. The situation was becoming impossible. She had to shake Stephen off. On impulse she spurted ahead through the crowd and came up on Louis' left. He glanced down at her enigmatically but he did not speak, and she felt suddenly foolish. From his other side Janine gave her a cool stare.

As they reached the open square where the dancing was to be held and began to fan out claiming tables, Rosalie felt a sense of hopelessness that was almost overwhelming. She must get away by herself. Away from Stephen; away from Louis and Janine. Looking around swiftly, she saw there was a small alleyway to the right. Surreptitiously, she slipped into the narrow space between the buildings. It was very dark here and the alley seemed endless. At last she came breathlessly to a corner and swung thankfully into a lamplit street where trailing geraniums grew down from the gardens of the small, white, boxy villas above.

Everything had gone wrong, she thought unhappily as she wandered along, kicking little stones with her toes, and there was no one to blame but herself. She had been foolish to come to Mykonos without formulating a plan. It had been stupid of her to think something would come up by which she could pay Louis back for what he had done to Fay. What could she do other than let him down, which meant she would have to run out on her job? And she knew she would never do that; never do anything that would make her despise herself.

You're hiding from the truth, she told herself fiercely. There had been a plan from the beginning and, looking into her heart, she knew that she had spoiled it. Between a man and a woman there could be a situation where rules did not apply. All's fair in love and war, it was said. She had, she admitted to herself now, been going to make Louis fall in love with her. Then she would have thrown him aside as ruthlessly as he had thrown Fay. But it had all gone wrong from the start because his diabolical attraction had been too strong for her. She had not dared to allow herself even to simulate an attraction, for something told her, some deep and rather frightened voice inside her, that should she allow this situation to arise, there would be no turning back.

Now there was the wretched Janine clinging to his arm, hanging on his every word. How he laps it up, she thought bitterly. What flame would be added to the fire of his conceit if she should try, even pretending, to get his attention! And anyway, there was Stephen, liable at any moment to drop his innocent bomb by mentioning Fay.

There was only one thing to do, she decided, gritting her teeth, lifting her small chin. She must forget what she had come for. Fend Stephen off as best she could without arousing his antagonism, and ignore Louis. Concentrate on the job, for she was being paid well and it came naturally to her to be honest and to give of her best. Janine won't last, she told herself as she wandered along the twisting lanes in the silent night. Louis will go back to London in a few days, and then Janine will decide this job isn't really for her. He will be obliged to get me a more suitable assistant. And Stephen, after all, is only here for two weeks. I'll keep calm and try to be kind to him.

She felt better now that she had faced facts and worked things out for herself. I got into an emotional bog, she thought with a wry smile, and couldn't see the wood for the trees. She walked with a lighter step now, looking with interest at the little rocky gardens with their sprawling fig trees, their tough little rock plants with the bright flowers in pinks and yellows and hyacinth blue. Hyacinths. She wrinkled her forehead, remembering she was to have Greek myths and legends at her fingertips tomorrow when they went off to the sacred isle of Delos on Spiro's cousin's boat.

Wasn't it Apollo and a handsome youth called Hyacinthus, who was coveted by the god of the west wind, throwing the discus near Sparta? Ah, yes. The west wind in a jealous rage blew Apollo's discus so violently that it mortally wounded Hyacinthus. Drops of his blood were changed into a cluster of blue flowers the Greeks later called hyacinths. An unusually pretty tale, for Greek legends tended toward violence. The great god Zeus seemed always to be pursuing people with thunderbolts, splitting heads open, swallowing newborn babies. Ugh!

She walked and walked. An hour passed, perhaps two, before she retraced her footsteps and began to make her way up the roughly surfaced little lane that led to the villas. They lay in the moonlight stark white, with their great banks of bougainvillea dark as blood. Such a beautiful scene! Such a heavenly interlude this could have been, if only . . .

She had stepped onto the terrace and was taking the front-door key from her handbag when a harsh voice from the vine shade said, "So! And there you are."

Rosalie started as though one of Zeus' thunderbolts had indeed hit her. "What are you doing here?" she demanded, not understanding why she should react so aggressively.

"When one of my staff, for whom I am responsible, disappears in the flash of an eyelid without having the courtesy to say where she is going, what am I supposed to do?" asked Louis, rising and advancing toward her, his face dark with anger. "Sit down and enjoy my drinks and the dancing? Forget about the possibility that she might be in trouble?"

"So you plunked yourself down on the terrace and waited for the body to turn up," Rosalie retorted with a sarcastic laugh. "Some guardian angel you are." She heard the harsh sound of his indrawn breath as he reacted to her accusation. His hands clamped down like iron on her slim shoulders and in fury and exasperation he gave her a shake.

"What do you think I've been doing for the past hour and a half? I've climbed this hill twice. And I was just about to go back again and scatter our guests through the streets on an all-out hunt when I saw you coming. Wandering casually up that hill," he exploded, "as though nothing had happened."

"Nothing had happened," she shouted at him over the chattering of her teeth. "I went for a walk, that's all. I'm entitled to do that. You don't own me. How was I to know anyone would miss me? Particularly you," she spat at him, "twined as you were around

140

that useless doll Janine. And while we're on the subject," she flared, "you'd better take her back to England with you. I'll willingly do double the work. I'm doing it anyway. It's not f-f-fair to enc-c-courage her to dress up like a f-fashion model—" She was unable to go on.

"Dear me," said Louis in a voice resonant with surprise, "do I detect a little green-eyed monster looking over your shoulder?"

"Don't be stupid," she shouted at him, dashing the tears from her eyes with the back of her hand.

"Here, have a handkerchief." He reached out and with surprising gentleness began to wipe her cheeks. Roughly, she brushed his hand away. "Don't come near me again. After the way you treated Fay I wouldn't touch you with a barge pole. You're ruthless and callous—"

"Oh, yes," Louis replied impassively. "Ruthless and callous. I meant to warn you that voices carry well in this clear air. When talking about people behind their backs it's advisable to ensure you do it inside, with the doors closed." He gave her a blistering look. "And as to the way I treated Fay Oliver, perhaps there are a few things you should know—"

"Fay's dead. Don't you dare lie to me about her," stormed Rosalie, beside herself with anger and despair at the memory. "Don't you dare say a word against her. It's vile and evil to run people down when there's no way they can put the record straight. When they're d-d-dead."

There was silence for a long moment, and then Louis asked quietly, "What's Fay to you?" and waited.

"She was my sister," Rosalie blurted out brokenly. "Her father married my mother. We were brought up together. I know we are alike—just a bit—although we're not blood relations. Mostly, it's our voices. That's why you thought you had met me before. And you saw me in the—" She choked at the memory of that diabolical word *Forgiveness* he had had the nerve to write on the card he left with flowers on Fay's grave. "You didn't love her," she accused him. "How could you, and throw her out like that carrying your child?" The tears were burning behind her eyes. She could no longer see his face. "I loved her dearly. Th-there were only the three of us. Our grandmother, Fay, and me. Now, because of you, there's only Gran and—" The storm of emotion brought tears to pour down her face.

Gradually, she became aware of an incredible stillness and then Louis' voice saying, "Rosalie, Rosalie . . . please. I'm sorry."

She turned and rushed blindly toward her room, hit the front door with a crash, and fell back, her face numb with the impact, stars flying through her head. As she reeled his arms came around her gently and he helped her into a chair. She was vaguely aware that he was rummaging in her bag for the key, unlocking the door. Then he swept her up and carried her to her room. He laid her down on the bed, then hurried out. There was the sound of a tap running, and a moment later he was holding a wet cloth to her forehead.

"You'll have to stop ignoring doors," he said in a strange, distant voice. "They're formidable when closed and dangerous when open."

She turned her face to the wall so that she could not see him. After a little while he went away and misery like a black cloud engulfed her. Well, now he knew. She had made a fine mess of things, there was no doubt.

She drifted into a troubled sleep and dreamed of Fay. Fay, with her laughing, beautiful face, holding out a hand to Stephen, beckoning to him, sliding around a corner out of Rosalie's sight, laughing again, softly this time, until the sound wafted away on the breeze.

It was one of the guests who wakened her in the morning, apologetically. She stood looking down at Rosalie, still in the clothes she had worn the night before. "I'm so sorry," the girl said. "Louis asked me to tell you everything's ready for the picnic. My! You have got some bruise!"

Dazedly, Rosalie pulled herself into an upright position. The events of the night before came flooding blackly into her mind. With probing fingers she examined the lump on her forehead.

"Louis said you've been working terribly hard," the girl remarked sympathetically. Then she grinned. "You should have seen the luscious Janine rushing around—well, not quite rushing, but certainly putting her best foot forward this morning. Breakfast has all been cleared away, so you've only got to get your own and come down to the waterfront. We're going now because there's a bit of excitement there. A cruise liner has come in. I expect you'll be glad of the peace."

"You're all very kind," murmured Rosalie, feeling desperately conscience-stricken. She scrambled to her feet and looked at herself in the mirror. The bruise on her forehead was yellow and black and there was a nasty lump. She made for the bathroom, her head throbbing as she moved.

When she emerged from her room a little while later in shorts and a halter top she was surprised to see one of the terrace tables neatly set and Janine, dressed in a bikini, leaning back in a painted chair, idly filing her nails.

"Hello," she greeted Rosalie, giving her a curious

143

look. "So, what did happen last night?" Her eyes were pointedly on the lump that Rosalie had tried, without much success, to hide with her hair.

"I walked into a door. It was kind of you to allow me to sleep late."

"Oh, I didn't allow it," the other girl replied airily. "You were left undisturbed on Louis' explicit instructions. That's why I didn't really believe you had walked into a door. I thought there must be more to the story than that."

"Thank you for laying out my breakfast," said Rosalie, ignoring her insinuations. She went into the kitchen for coffee, feeling somewhat at a loss as she always was in the company of the glamorous, smoothly sophisticated Janine. I'm the one with the important job, she reminded herself sternly. I'm in charge. And yet this girl had the power to throw her completely off balance. She looked down at her neat little sky-blue shorts with a plain halter top in a darker shade, and grimaced. She must fight this inferiority complex Janine gave her. She must overcome her vulnerability.

The coffee was ready. She poured it into the mug. Returning, she commented, "I'm surprised to see you here. You don't have to wait for me, you know."

"I'm not waiting for you," Janine replied, looking suddenly like the cat that has swallowed the cream. "I'm waiting for Louis to come back. We're not going to Delos. We're going to spend the day over at Platiyalos. Or maybe on the nudist beach," she added provocatively, eyes slanted, holding up one hand for inspection. "See what has happened to my poor nails? They're practically nonexistent now."

"When you take on a job as cook and bottle washer you've got to have the right nails for it," Rosalie snapped and received a supercilious stare in return.

"If that's how you see yourself," Janine said patronizingly, "don't count me in!"

"If you came as anything else, then you came under false pretenses," Rosalie told her, hating herself for being so cross but unable to hold back the bitter words. Janine merely shrugged with the air of one who doesn't need to worry about lesser mortals.

Rosalie ate her breakfast swiftly, scarcely tasting it. Then she washed up her dishes, took a crocheted string bag she had bought at a crafts stall in the market, and threw some things into it: a pencil and notebook, a comb, tissues, a first-aid kit for scraped knees (someone was bound to slip on a rock), some aspirins for the inevitable headache produced by the relentless sun (people had to learn by experience, she already knew, to wear their hats), and a map of Delos which she had bought in the town, showing the layout of the various archaeological sites and pinpointing those of the old Roman villas that had survived their long past.

"Goodbye," she said civilly to Janine, clamping her little straw hat on her head as she went across the terrace where the other girl still reclined. "I hope you have a nice day."

"And you," replied Janine graciously. "I'm sure I will," she added with total confidence and that feline smile.

Rosalie forced jauntiness into her step as she descended the hill to the town. Thank goodness, after what had happened last night, she did not have to face Louis. So he was taking Janine to the nudist beach! Good luck to them, she thought cuttingly, if that's what they want. And if he treated Janine the way he treated Fay . . . well, that was her problem.

Down on the waterfront tourists were walking excitedly around, exclaiming with delight at the shawls, the beads, the miniature windmills displayed outside curio shops. Dark-skinned fishermen in black caps sitting outside tavernas played their games of backgammon imperturbably. Groups of young men argued on street corners in the time-honored Greek way.

Spiro's cousin Nicholas had the caïque ready, tied up to the little jetty. It was an old fishing boat, rough and ready and still smelling a little of its past. The sides were striped in harsh Greek colors—green, brick, ocher. Sturdily built and safe, it rocked on the choppy waters, disturbed by the busy little launches leaving off passengers from the cruise ship. Rosalie saw with gratitude that the big lunch basket was already settled amidships. Somebody (Louis?) had been very kind.

Nicholas came hurrying forward, stepping warily over the ropes that lay on the ground.

"Ah! There you are," he greeted her, looking pleased, almost proprietorial. "Louis is not coming," he said, and Rosalie saw immediately that that was the reason for his lightheartedness. "I am going to have you all to myself."

"You and seventeen others," she retorted before she could stop herself. Oh, why did she have to be so angry today? she asked herself. The bruise on her forehead wasn't hurting at all now. She had absolutely no excuse. And besides, wasn't she being paid to be a pleasant hostess? She forced herself to smile and at the same time put a gentle hand on Nicholas' arm. "I'm the guide, that's all I meant," she said apologetically.

The guests had seen her arrival and were approaching across the white-ringed cobblestones. They looked colorful and happy in their casual clothes as they exchanged pleasantries with one another, comparing sunburns from the day before and greeting Rosalie.

"What a bruise!"

"Did you really walk into a door, or were you molested by an amorous Greek?"

"What happened last night? Why did you leave the dancing?"

"She got in the way of one of Zeus' thunderbolts." The familiar voice with its ring of authority brought forth delighted laughter. Rosalie turned away, not wanting to look at Louis.

"Come on," he ordered. "All aboard. Where are the stragglers? Two, four, six, eight—you're all here. Look after them, Nico. No accidents, mind."

"My caïque is unsinkable, Meester Louis, you know that. All Greek caïques unsinkable," the handsome Greek averred. "Now, beautiful Mees Darrien, I help you in."

"You may call me Rosalie," Rosalie told him, smiling, and feeling that block of ice deep down within her melting a little at his compliment. She wanted Louis to see him flirting with her.

"Rosalie." He turned the name over on his tongue, shortening the *o*, stretching out the *e* at the end, making it sound pretty and foreign. Rosalie smiled at him again. The guests were tumbling into the caïque, trying to catch the little vessel on an upward swell, jostling each other, laughing.

"I want the bow."

"You'll get sprayed when we strike the open sea."

"I don't mind. In this hot sun I'll soon dry."

Louis was standing beside her. She could sense his presence without actually seeing him. To her chagrin, her knees began to tremble.

"Have a nice day," she said coldly, wishing her

voice had not taken on that bleak cadence again, feeling the warmth slide out of her as she looked at Louis' hard face.

Louis thrust his hands into his pockets, and again she felt that uprush of awareness of him. His animal strength. His tremendous sexuality. "You, too. I'm sorry I'm not coming, but you wouldn't want to spoil a picnic on a romantic mountain by having to share it with someone who is ruthless and callous," he said lightly. "I can spare you that and at the same time have a very pleasant day myself."

She looked up and their eyes met. His were dark, unreadable behind their sooty lashes. Her own faltered and swung away. How she despised him. She turned and prepared to enter the caïque with Nicholas gallantly supporting her. Stephen helped her to the seat he had saved in the stern. She gave him a brief smile of resignation. Nicholas entered the wheelhouse and started the engine.

Chapter Ten

As they left the harbor the little gray islands that dotted the Aegean rose to view and Rosalie dutifully began her tourist spiel. "That's Rheneia, that stony lump on the starboard side," she told her passengers, shouting over the noise of the engine. "After Apollo's birth on Delos the Athenians decreed that the island should be sacred and no one thereafter was to be born or to die there. So they sent pregnant women, sick people, and old people to Rheneia. They even carried out purifications by removing all human remains that were buried there."

Stephen said, "You're a mine of information."

"It wasn't difficult to study up. Louis provided the guidebooks."

"Louis," Stephen said thoughtfully, looking at her as though trying to read her mind. "What actually did happen last night?"

"Please, Stephen," she begged him, irritated by his persistence. "I've got a job to do."

He said peevishly, "You didn't seem to be doing much of a job last night when you disappeared from the dancing."

"I went for a walk," Rosalie replied shortly. "I wasn't on duty."

"I thought you were on duty twenty-four hours a day."

She did not like being pinned down like this. What she did was not his business, but she kept her indignation under control. "There was nothing I could do to help anyone. It was a purely social evening."

"That's how it seemed for both of you," he replied meaningfully, "when suddenly Louis wasn't there either. And this morning we're told to keep quiet and allow you to sleep. Then you turn up with a hefty bruise on your forehead. I didn't come down in the last shower, you know," he said spitefully.

She put a hand up to shield her mouth, seething. "People are listening," she whispered.

"People are curious," he said heavily. "They're being polite, but I can tell you, they are curious. You and Louis alone last night and Janine in a fury, and now Janine and Louis off, if one can believe that girl, to cavort au naturel on the nudists' beach today. I grant you Louis is a very attractive man, but do you really want to make a fool of yourself?"

Burning with humiliation, Rosalie clambered to her feet. Stepping carefully, she made her way to the wheelhouse. Nico greeted her with a flash of beautiful white teeth. "You come to keep me company, Ros-a-lee," he said happily, making way for her. She smiled at him, swallowing the hard anger she felt at Stephen's insinuations, which were all the more painful, she had to admit to herself, for being true. Luckily, a caïque

150

passed on the port side, causing a diversion when the passengers saw that it carried several cows and half a dozen goats standing patiently amidships as though well accustomed to this form of travel.

Rosalie took the opportunity to resume her job as guide and, standing outside the wheelhouse, she informed the passengers, "The islands are used for grazing, and caïques are the only means of transport from one island to another. If you keep an eye out you'll probably see some dolphins, too." Almost immediately there was a cry of delight from a girl in the bow. "Look!" They all looked and there was a school of dolphins, their dark bodies glittering in the sun as they leaped high in the air. Rosalie managed to impart her little pieces of information while studiously avoiding catching Stephen's eye.

They went ashore at Delos. Those who had sat in the bow were wet from the spray that flew up as the little vessel forged her way through the choppy sea, but they were happy, professing themselves to be cooler than the rest of the party. Rosalie gathered everyone together, explaining that she would first of all take them to the excavated houses of rich merchants, where they could see marble pillars and mosaic floors. "You probably all know the island was the center of trade between East and West before the birth of Christ." They nodded interestedly. They were going to be a good audience, she thought, gratified. She hoped they would help her forget her problems for a few hours.

She led the party along the dry, dusty earth paths where scarlet poppies, wild marrow, and sea lavender grew. Little brown lizards scuttled out of their way, drawing cries of delight from everyone. "Over there," she told them, pointing to a dried-out basin surrounded by a low stone wall, "is the Sacred Lake."

"Not much of a lake," commented one of the party.

"No, in 1926 the stream that ran down from Mount Cynthus ran dry, and since then archaeologists have been tossing the soil from the diggings into what was the lake. That's Mount Cynthus behind. We're going to climb up there for lunch. Nicholas and some of his boatmen friends are going to transport the food while you're on your culture jaunt."

"Just as well we don't have to do it," said one of the men, flapping his hands at flies that hovered around his face. Then someone saw the palm tree and uttered a cry. "I don't believe it!"

Rosalie smiled. "Some archaeologists with a fine sense of romance planted another palm on the spot where Apollo was said to have been born."

"That's nice." And they all agreed. She took them down the Sacred Way, a dusty avenue that led to the famous row of marble lions standing nobly on their plinths, heads high as they had stood through the centuries. "Some of them are rather damaged, you will see," she told her listeners, "but what can you expect from statues that have been exposed to the weather for nearly fourteen hundred years?"

"They're wonderful!"

"Marvelous."

The group split up and wandered in and out among the plinths, gazing in awe at the great white beasts. The sun was scorching now, the heat beating up from the stones. Rosalie kept easing her hat back onto the crown of her head, wiping her damp forehead.

"You've done your homework very well," said Stephen at her elbow. "May I walk with you? I'm sorry I made you cross. It's just that—I was so looking forward to being with you last night. I felt resentful when you and Alexander disappeared."

Rosalie managed a brief smile. She would cut off

her hand rather than hurt him after what he had been through. Louis has all this to answer for, she thought bitterly. Louis, who was idling the day away in the sun with the lovely Janine. "You look like a wood nymph," said Stephen, "with no hair showing and no makeup."

Nymph! The word struck at her heart. Louis had called her that. "Don't be silly," she flared before she could stop herself. "Leave me alone, Stephen. Leave me alone. I'm here on a job and . . ." Her voice trailed off, for he had fallen behind, crushed at her rejection. How could she have done that to him? And only a moment ago she had been thinking she would rather cut off her right hand. . . . Oh, dear, she said to herself confusedly. She didn't seem to understand herself anymore.

They went down the Sacred Way and Rosalie showed them Apollo's temple. Then a sanctuary with a near-perfect mosaic floor surrounded by marble stumps that once were elegant Doric columns.

"Mithridates and his army were responsible for this devastation in 88 B.C.," she told them. "Those broken pillars were made of the finest Parian marble."

They picked their way among the remains of the pillars that lay on the ground, listening interestedly to the snippets of ancient history Rosalie gave them. A sigh of relief went up when she suggested they find the coffee shop and have a drink before starting the long trail up Mount Cynthus. Already they had been dehydrated by the blazing sun.

They wandered into the shop and looked around for seats. Penitently, Rosalie followed Stephen. Sitting beside him, she gave him a small, tentative smile. "Bear with me, Stephen. You clearly don't find the situation as complex as I do."

"What are you referring to?" he asked uncertainly.

"I'm talking about us. Fay and you and me."

He heaved a sigh. "I'd like to talk about Fay. You've never allowed me to. I'd like to explain my side. And apologize for dr—for what I did to you. You've never even allowed me to do that."

"I don't want to talk about Fay. She's dead." Their guests were glancing up at them, then tactfully looking away. One or two of them exchanged knowing looks. Rosalie bristled with embarrassment.

"You didn't know her," said Stephen.

"I lived with her since we were children," Rosalie retorted indignantly. "How could I not know her?"

He ran a hand distractedly through his fair hair. "I'm trying to tell you you *didn't* know her. You're right, Rosalie. She is dead. And so it's the turn of the living now. I want to talk to you about what she did to me. I want to exorcise her. She lies between us."

Rosalie jumped up. "You fell in love with her, Stephen," she said in a quick, distant little voice. "I find that perfectly understandable. I'll get our drinks. What do you want? Coffee? Coke? Tea?"

He flopped back in his chair, looking resigned. "Okay. Wait on me." There was a shadow of a smile on his face. "With twelve days to go, I'm not giving up hope."

They finished their drinks, then trudged up the dry, stony track in the heat. Stephen stayed at her side. Again she felt faintly irritated by the way the others left them alone and by the surreptitious looks people gave them. Of course there would be gossip. Good-naturedly, everyone wanted them to get together again. When they reached the summit Nicholas their boatman was there with two Greek friends, smiling a welcome. They settled wearily where they could find seats, on stones that were really too hot for comfort and on dry grass. Rosalie unpacked the hamper.

154

Stephen, falling easily into the role of host, poured the wine. "It's room temperature," he joked, and they all laughed. "Some hot room!"

The Greeks settled comfortably among them to eat their salami and rolls and feta cheese. They shared a bottle of unlabeled wine, drinking it from the bottle, laughing gustily at the others for using plastic cups.

"Penny," said Stephen at her side. "They must be nice, to produce that dreamy smile."

Rosalie flushed scarlet, turning her head away as though she feared he might read her thoughts. There had been a picture in her mind of Louis, who had intended to accompany them today, leaning casually against a boulder, his chest bare where the shirt fell back unbuttoned, drinking from the bottle. Like the peasants, yet not like them except that the lusty side of him showed. She said confusedly, "I was simply thinking—thinking—what a blissful view. Those little islands—like crouching mice."

Nicholas said expansively, "I will take you to all of them. Any one you like," he amended when they laughed. "Of course there are too many." And the awkward moment with Stephen passed.

They finished the lunch, and Nicholas packed away the empty bottles, the plastic bags and cups.

"Let's not go back to the ruins," suggested one of the guests, spread-eagled on the rough ground. "It's too hot. Let's make Rosalie tell us stories while we gaze at the view."

"Who was Eros' father?" asked the girl called Nan.

Rosalie's soft mouth turned down wryly. "That's the sixty-four-thousand-dollar question. Hermes? Poseidon? Dionysus? Or somebody else? Aphrodite was a very promiscuous goddess and a bit hard to tie down, since she could renew her virginity in the sea." She told them some of the legends, suiting her voice

155

and her information to their light holiday mood. They did not want to be instructed seriously. They wanted to sunbathe and laugh and tease her. "Eros shot golden arrows at random to make people fall in love." There was a burst of delighted laughter and Rosalie glanced around, following the group's eyes with a questioning glance. Stephen's hands were raised, simulating a hold on a crossbow, his eyes narrowed on her. She jumped up, hiding her anger at their good-natured raillery as best she could. "Why don't we make Nicholas take us around to the Sacred Bay in the caïque for a swim?"

Lazily, they climbed to their feet. "Okay, that's not a bad idea." They wandered off in little groups. Again Rosalie attempted to join a group, but the guests paused in surprise, waiting for Stephen to catch up. She heaved a long sigh. I may as well resign myself to the situation she thought despairingly. I seem to be stuck with him. The two weeks will pass and he will have to go home.

They arrived back at Mykonos as the sun was going down. Tourists and locals alike were gathering at the little tables outside the tavernas for the evening apéritif. "Let me buy you an ouzo," said Stephen at her elbow.

"Thanks, but I must get back. I've got a job to do, remember?"

"We're eating out tonight; there's nothing for you to do."

"There's always the situation of being on duty," she retorted. And then, before he could offer to accompany her, she said, "Please stay with the others, Stephen."

He gave her a straight look. "Louis will be at the villas."

"So will Janine. Oh, for heaven's sake, Stephen,

156

what makes you think I'm attracted to that man? He's arrogant, chauvinistic, and—"

"And you love it," retorted Stephen, sounding bruised. "Perhaps I should ill-treat you a bit. Perhaps you'd like me better."

She was too annoyed to remind him that he had already done that when he dropped her for Fay. Besides, she had vowed not to hurt him. She swung on her heel and turned up the street.

Louis and Janine were seated at a table on the terrace. The first thought to strike Rosalie was that they must have been back some time, because they were dressed for the evening. Janine wore a jump suit in a startling shade of purple that fell seductively across her bosom and left her back bare. There were silver necklaces at her throat, and she wore silver sandals. Her glossy black hair fell softly around her shoulders in luxuriant waves, and her skin had picked up an enviable, even tan.

Louis rose. "How did the day go?" He stood looking down at her, his golden eyes soft, she assumed, from the happiness of the day, his skin shades darker than it had been in the morning and without a trace of burn.

"Very satisfactory," she replied coolly, fighting his magnetism, turning away to face Janine. "And you?"

"Utter bliss," cooed Janine, giving Louis a seductive look. "I'm sorry yours was only satisfactory. You did have Stephen, but of course you also had a crowd. Poor you." She smoothed the soft folds of her jump suit over one hip, eyeing Louis again with a private look, as though they had secrets between them.

"I'd better go and change." She crossed the terrace beneath the massed pink bougainvillea blossoms and entered the villa. Her tiny room looked bare and unfriendly. She caught a glimpse of herself in the mirror and glanced quickly away. The tip of her nose was burned, her shorts were grubby, and her hair was a tangled blond mass from immersion in the seawater. She suddenly felt tired and inexpressibly lonely. It was stupid of her to have taken this job. You didn't pay back men like Louis. He was a born winner. She slipped out of her shorts and top and, wrapping a towel around herself sarong fashion, headed for the bathroom.

The fresh, soft water felt wonderful. She shampooed her hair and scrubbed the sand from between her toes. The overflow pipe played one of its Greek tricks and sent the waste water up through the grating in the floor. She gave a little sigh of annoyance. With her wet towel draped around her and her hair dripping down her back, she splashed blindly out into the hall and bumped into Louis. His hand descended on her shoulder. She felt the towel slip and made a grab for it. One end evaded her grasp and slid to the floor. There was a terrible moment when she stood before him stark naked, and then she had grabbed the errant material and, scarlet with humiliation, dashed for her room. As she slammed the door there was an echo of Louis' soft laugh. For several moments, curled up like a small animal on the foot of her bed, she gave herself up to despair. There was a knock on the door. "Go away," she said through gritted teeth.

A plaintive voice inquired, "What on earth happened in the bathroom?"

"It's flooded," Rosalie retorted angrily. "Get Louis to unblock it."

"He's gone. The water's running into the hall."

"Then clean it up, please," retorted Rosalie, her spirit returning, knowing she was being unfair. Not caring.

"Why should I clean up a mess you made?" Janine asked resentfully.

Rosalie leaped off the bed and, holding the towel fiercely around her, flung the door open. "Because you were hired to assist me," she flared, her eyes dangerous. "I didn't make the mess. It was caused by inefficient plumbing."

Janine looked at her as though she could not believe her ears. "This isn't my villa,' she said uncertainly.

"They're all your villas, all three, just as they're all my responsibility," Rosalie retorted. "There's a mop in the kitchen cupboard." She retired to her room feeling spent and tearful. But it only lasted a moment. Pulling herself together, feeling desperately ashamed, she picked up a dry towel and wrapped it around her head, took a pair of trousers and a plain tailored blouse from a drawer, and slipped into them. She emerged a moment later neatly attired, with the turban still around her head and sandals on her feet.

Janine was standing in the hall in her beautiful outfit holding a mop, carefully keeping her silver slippers out of the flood. "You're more suitably dressed than I am for this," she said resentfully.

Rosalie took the mop and swished the water back into the bathroom. Janine watched her. Suddenly, looking at the silver necklaces, the silver slippers, the beautiful jump suit, the anger in Rosalie boiled up and spilled over. Leaning on the mop, she said, using tremendous effort to keep her voice even, "Since you're admitting you're not suitably dressed for the job you've taken on, I suggest you change. Louis put me in charge and I've been very fair with you. I've given you several days to settle in and get the feel of the place. You're not a guest. You're staff. I'm sorry to have to point this out, but since the fact seems to have escaped you, I'm forced to do so. From now on, you're to take orders from me. I want you to dress suitably in future. And I want you to be prepared to do what I tell you to do."

Janine looked at Rosalie with hatred darkening her beautiful eyes. "I thought we were to share the work."

"So did I," replied Rosalie. "But in two days and two nights you haven't offered to share anything."

"I got breakfast this morning while you slept late," Janine pointed out virtuously.

Rosalie felt herself deflating under the very fair accusation, but she held her ground. "So you did, with a great deal of help from good-natured guests. But that's not allowed anymore. Those are my terms. If you don't like them, tell Louis. I am sure he'll release you. I'll tell him I can manage very well myself until he gets a replacement. And by the way," she added, "do you speak Greek?"

The girl nodded, but her eyes were uncertain. "Just a few words."

"How many words?" Rosalie asked, speaking in Greek. Janine flushed. It was clear she had not understood. "I only know some restaurant Greek," she admitted. "Like . . ." She met Rosalie's stormy eyes and glanced away, her voice trailing off.

"Like the words you can learn parrot fashion from a phrase book?" Rosalie asked scathingly.

"I suppose so."

"So you took the job under false pretenses?"

"Well—I mean—you won't tell Louis, will you?"

Rosalie felt almost sorry for her. "If Louis wanted to know he would know already. Now I think we're clear where we stand. By the way, you can take responsibility for dinner tonight. I've been on duty all day."

"Responsibility?" echoed the other girl, and Rosalie thought by the way her beautiful face fell that she had hoped to dine alone with Louis. "What do you mean?"

"There's nothing to do except see that Spiro gives the party good service and comes up with the menu promised," Rosalie told her crisply.

"Oh, yes, yes, of course." The water was already receding down the grille, righting itself in the way Rosalie knew so well from previous jobs on Corfu and Kos. A mere idiosyncrasy of Greek plumbing.

"Tell Louis I am having dinner alone tonight."

"You're not allowed to," Janine said resentfully. "I heard Louis say you're on duty twenty-four hours a day."

"Well, it's going to be twenty hours today," Rosalie replied sweetly. "Tell Louis that, if you like."

Chapter Eleven

Rosalie went back into her room feeling shaken by the ordeal. But it had had to be said, she told herself. Janine would undoubtedly report the scene to Louis. And if Louis wanted to fire her, that was okay by her, too, she told herself defensively. She would be glad to get out. She unwrapped the towel from her head, rubbed her hair dry, and combed it out. In the mirror her eyes were still stormy, her cheeks flushed. It was too late now for a long walk on the stony hills, for dusk had fallen, but she needed to work off the pressures of the day. She flung her shoulder bag over her arm and left the villa by the back entrance, walking up to the pretty windmill.

She stood on the knoll looking down over the town, feeling drained from the fracas with Janine but glad, very glad, that she had gone through with it. What made me do it? she asked herself and could not answer. But some part of her knew. Somewhere, deep down in her heart, she was aware of a primitive survival instinct that had come to her defense when she saw Louis and Janine sitting together on the terrace with the sun going down. Looking warmed by whatever the day had held for them. Two beautiful people, clearly so right for each other.

Lights were springing up everywhere like glow-worms, and down on the harbor a necklace of gold marked the curve of the bay. The big cruise ship still lay at anchor bejeweled with lights from bow to stern, each deck ablaze and all the portholes glowing. She thought of the fun going on there, visualizing rich male tourists and beautifully gowned women chatting in the colorful lounges, imbibing drinks at friendly get-togethers in the bars. She had never felt so alone.

She lifted her chin, turned her back on the loveliness, and set out down the narrow path that led between cactus and dry shrubs to the little beach where she had met Louis the other day and where they had had their swim. There was barely enough light to see. When she came to the stairs she had to step in gingerly fashion to avoid falling. At the bottom she took the path that led to the beach, climbed over a low wall, and crossed the stones to where golden sand edged the water. The sea murmured gently as it rose and fell. There was a salty tang here and the musty, piquant smell of seaweed. The moon was not yet risen. A pearl-pink shadow lay on the horizon where the sun had gone down.

The sand seeping through her open sandals was pleasantly cool. Rosalie wandered around the little bay and clambered over the rocks. It was almost dark now, but she had grown accustomed to the failing light and could see well enough. The streetlights behind gave her bearings. She found another path that ran into a lane behind some houses and strode up it, relishing the exercise. Some of the passion in her still needed to be worked off. She came to some more steps, overhung with a vine of lovely yellow bell-like flowers that glowed palely in the light of a streetlamp. She passed several little white chapels heavily padlocked as they always were. An old peasant woman in black sitting on a hard chair on a balcony close to the road gave her a gap-toothed smile.

She walked on and on, scarcely noticing where she was going or how the time passed, but aware that the restiveness, the unhappiness, was falling away as her energy flagged. She knew she was walking in circles, occasionally touching the edge of the little town, then turning back and traversing the outlying lanes where there were gardens and more trees. At last she paused and looked at her watch. It was nine o'clock and she was hungry.

She had seen a small outdoor restaurant on a rise farther back where the land fell away directly to the sea. It was safely distant from Spiro's—rather off the beaten track—so she was unlikely to come across any of the guests there. She backtracked and found it. There was only one table vacant. Thankfully, she sat down, stretching her aching legs. There were pots of geraniums dotted here and there, the flowers glowing red in the pale lamplight. It was pretty and restful. She sat back, briefly closing her eyes. A waiter came and smilingly set the table. "You are alone?" She answered him in Greek, wanting to be detached from her Englishness. He looked surprised at first and then delighted. "Where did you learn to speak our language?"

"Working in the islands."

"I will bring you the Greek menu."

164

"Please don't," she protested, smiling. "I can't read Greek."

"Okay." She turned her chair a little so that she could look directly out to sea. The cruise ship's funnels emitted an earsplitting blast and the vessel began to move through the darkness. When the waiter returned she ordered moussaka, that delicious concoction of eggplant, mincemeat, red wine, cheese, and spices. "And you would like some wine?" The waiter had reverted to Greek again. Rosalie shook her head.

"Yes, thank you," said a familiar voice behind her, speaking also in Greek. "A bottle of Demestica. And two ouzos to start."

Rosalie swung around, automatically leaping to her feet.

"Sorry to startle you," Louis said soothingly. "Do sit down again." He pulled out a chair for himself.

"I'd really rather like a quiet meal alone," Rosalie managed to say coolly, though she was suddenly shaking inside. "And I don't want a drink."

"You've been alone quite long enough," Louis retorted imperturbably, "and a drink will do you good." He leaned back in his chair, his arrogant head lifted so that the lamplight touched it softly, the hard mouth smiling.

"How did you find me?" It was very suspicious, Rosalie thought, irritated, that he should turn up the very moment she found a restaurant.

"I didn't find you, I've been following you for some time," he replied outrageously. "I always thought people got a creepy feeling when they were being followed. Very insensitive of you not to have noticed." Those tawny eyes were dancing, the mouth flicking up at the corners. Before she could answer, two ouzos arrived. He picked up the jug of water and

165

added some to her drink, clouding it prettily, but took his own straight. "Cheers. I should have thought climbing Mount Cynthus was enough exercise for the average mortal," he said. "Have you really been walking since you left the villa? And if so, why?" He held her glass of watered-down ouzo out so that she had to take it.

Reluctantly, she ventured a sip. It was considerably less fiery this way. "Didn't Janine tell you?" she inquired cautiously.

"That you suddenly took up the reins? Yes, she did." His eyes glimmered golden in that way they had when he was amused. "You haven't given me an answer, though. I asked why you were walking up and down the lanes all alone in the dark. Not surely because I saw your beautiful body. A Psyche, alone and unadorned." She blushed crimson. "It is a beautiful body," he said softly.

She pulled herself together. She had to divert him from this embarrassing subject. "I was—I suppose—getting over the altercation. Coming to terms with— Er—I mean, it took a lot of courage to start pushing Janine around."

"Janine?" he asked, astonished, faintly amused. Then he was actually laughing and there was the haunting memory of days they had spent together swimming, working, becoming almost friends. "When I gave you the job I thought you were executive material."

She gulped at her drink. "Even executives think twice before giving orders to their managing director's girl friend." She looked away because she did not want to see the expression on his face.

"Oh," he said solemnly. "So that was it. Your moussaka has arrived. They make a particularly good one here." He turned the wineglasses over so that the waiter could fill them.

"I'm too hungry for wine," she demurred. "That ouzo really hit my empty stomach. I—I don't want to get drunk." She was remembering what had happened when they jumped out of the window of the nightclub together.

"It will do you good," he told her again. She dug her fork into the aromatic moussaka. "How is it?"

"Lovely. Superb. Wonderful." She felt her spirits lift.

"Have some more wine." He picked up the bottle.

She looked at him suspiciously. "What are you trying to do?"

"Loosen you up, of course," he replied with the unique magic in his smile that made her heart turn over. "I want to talk to you. We need to be friends."

"We can never be friends." She blurted the words out.

"Because of Fay? Don't answer that. Finish your meal. You've had a bad day. That idiot Barrington's getting on your nerves, isn't he?" And without waiting for an answer he said, "You'd never marry him. You might have thought about it, but you'd never do it, I'll warrant."

Rosalie felt she needed the protection Stephen's name could give. "I—I owe him a lot," she murmured.

"Why?" Louis thrust his face close to hers. "Has Barrington been so good to you?"

She looked away, but by the very power of his personality he drew her eyes back to him. "It—it's something I can't discuss."

"Don't let it spoil your dinner. This is splendid wine. Possibly the best in Greece. It comes from the

Peloponnese. I'll take you there sometime," Louis promised with his rare smile. "Olympia, home of the gods. A beautiful, romantic, leafy place. A fitting place for the gods," he said dreamily.

The food was beginning to stick in Rosalie's throat. She put her fork down. "I can never go anywhere with you," she said. Her eyes were clouded and there was a choking sensation in her throat.

Momentarily, his own eyes grew dark, and then he said lightly, "Finish your dinner or I shall be forced to spoon-feed you, and you'd find that embarrassing in public. Let's not talk about tricky subjects, shall we? Not until after coffee, anyway. Look, there's that cruise liner making out to sea. They've all seen beautiful Mykonos—the passengers, and even some of the crew—and now they're comparing miniature windmills and vases of flowers made of shells and going down to dinner in new cottons from the boutiques with new woolen shawls draped over their shoulders to keep the air conditioning out."

Rosalie ate in silence, listening to his patter with half an ear, forcing herself to think of Fay. Of the incredible waste of a life. Two lives for which Louis had been responsible and which he had thrown away. She must not allow his insidious charm to affect her. She had come to work for him with hate in her heart and she had weakly allowed him to divert her. But today she had found strength again. She had stood up to Janine, and now she would stand up to Louis. He was still talking, his eyes bright, his manner engaging, but she had scarcely heard the words. Something about the gods. Pandora's box, out of which she had allowed all the evils of the world to fly.

"Pandora's box," he repeated, and his eyes grew dark again as he mused.

Rosalie went stolidly on with her meal. Louis was silent, sipping at his drink. It was an oddly companionable silence. Rosalie finished. Suddenly, without warning, he asked, "Where did I meet you before?"

She sat back, pushing her empty plate away. "You never met me," she said. "You probably saw me in the churchyard the day of Fay's funeral. I mean, that evening." She added bitterly, "You hadn't the nerve to come and pay your respects earlier." Her voice was soft, scathing. "You crept in after everyone had gone and put an audacious card on the grave. It said *Forgiveness.*" She paused, looking at him, and he looked back at her with somber eyes. "You expected to be forgiven?" she asked, her voice savage, "after what you did to her? And your child?"

As she spoke his eyes narrowed to slits in his tanned face. The noble features became almost ugly with whatever was behind them. How she hated this man who had taken her beloved sister from her. With revulsion, she pushed her chair back and stood up, but suddenly his hand thrust out and he had her by the wrist, his grip like steel. "I loved her," he said. "That's why I put that card on the flowers. That's why I bothered to bring them. I loved her."

The waiter came with the bill on a saucer. Louis gave it a cursory glance, took some notes from his pocket with his free hand, and, scarcely looking at them, put them down on the plate. Still gripping her wrist, he led her off the little raised stone platform on which the tables sat. The waiter stared after them, shrugging.

They walked swiftly, in silence, up the road, Rosalie setting the pace, not noticing where she was going until suddenly there was a bank of vines in front of them, and darkness. Louis jerked her roughly around.

"My child?" His voice was harsh. "Why would she marry someone else, if she knew she was carrying my child?"

"Because it needed a father," Rosalie flared. "What did you expect her to do?"

He was silent, his hands gripping her shoulders cruelly. "I wouldn't expect her to marry a man who was not the father of the child," he said obscurely. "And he left her, didn't he? The death notice gave her maiden name. Why? Why did he leave?"

"Because he knew it couldn't possibly be his child. Why else?" she asked bitterly. And now that everything was out in the open she added miserably, "You may as well know, she married poor Stephen Barrington. That's why I have to be nice to him."

Louis did not answer, but she felt the shock go through him. "So he was the fall guy!" She heard the hiss of his indrawn breath. "Oh, what a mess!"

Rosalie jerked away. "Now you will understand when I say I loathe and despise you. I took your job under false pretenses. I meant to—I wanted to—pay you back, and—but—it's all gone wrong." There was a dry sob in her throat.

"Yes," Louis said softly. "It's all gone terribly, terribly wrong. We fell in love."

"How can you say that when you spent all day at the beach with Janine?" she shouted at him.

"Oh," he said, his voice still soft, "so that's it! Didn't I have to get Janine out of your hair? And a very successful ploy it was," he added exultantly. "It had the effect I had hoped for." As he came closer, closer, she stood like a trapped animal, her eyes on the hard, sensual lines of his mouth, fighting the rising tide of longing in her. Then his lips found hers, at first light and warm; then as the kiss took fire suddenly there was a despair and desire and a kind of madness in them both. His hands pressed into her spine and she yielded to him, flames of passion sending her senses reeling, the hot blood pounding in her ears. Even knowing she should be reeling away from him, she slid her hands up around his neck, sensuously caressing the muscles, the nape. Her fingertips were sliding through the silk of his wonderful black hair and a primitive shudder of excitement shook her whole being.

At last his arms relaxed and she moved away from him. There was something in his eyes that frightened her. A demand, and a promise. "It can never be like that for us," she cried wildly. "You'll not treat me the way you treated Fay. So you loved her, did you?" she asked bitterly, wiping the back of her hand across her mouth to rid herself of the poison and the wonder of his kisses. "You loved her so much you threw her out and she died of a broken heart."

He opened his mouth to say something violent. She could see the passion in his eyes and in the cruel line of his lips. But she would not listen. She flung herself out of reach, swung around, and ran. She ran back past the restaurant where the waiter stared after her in surprise, shrugging again over the craziness of youth. She ran down the empty street where a bouzouki wailed from an open door, and broke into the meandering evening crowds. Breathlessly, she dashed in and out among the old black-clad women, the old men, the tourists, and the small Greek children who ought to have been in bed long ago. She ran until she reached the waterfront, then turned breathlessly up the hill. There was no more strength in her then. Her body was damp with sweat and her newly washed silky hair clung to her neck. Gasping, she slowed to a walk, praying that Louis would not catch up.

171

They were all on the terrace sitting at the little tables as though outside a taverna, drinking wine and chatting. Someone had bought a bouzouki and was strumming it tentatively while a girl sang in a soft, sweet voice. They watched her approach, saw her flushed face and perhaps saw too the distress, for no one spoke. The girl stopped singing. Rosalie walked past them to the open front door. Janine was seated beside it dressed in trousers, flat-heeled sandals, and a tailored blouse. She gave Rosalie a curious, uncertain look. Rosalie went along the passage into her room and shut the door. Then she took the hard little kitchen chair on which she spread her clothes at night, pushed it under the doorknob, and fell onto her bed in a paroxysm of grief.

Rosalie wakened with a heavy heart, her eyes swollen from crying. It was half past six and the villa was silent. She dragged herself out of bed and looked in the mirror. "Ugh!" The burning sun of Delos had done its worst in spite of the fact that she had carefully kept her hat on her head. Her forehead was scarlet and her nose pink. She touched it gingerly, tentatively. It felt sore. She went along to the bathroom, her bare feet silent on the tiles. The shower was refreshing, but the water hit her face like spikes. She dressed in jeans and an old cotton blouse, rubbed some suntan lotion into her skin, and pinned her hair on top of her head. Who cared what she looked like? She went to the kitchen to pick up the basket in which she carried the bread.

There was a card leaning against the coffeepot. *Taken an early plane to London. Confident you will cope. Ring office if in trouble. Louis.* Rosalie stood looking at the note for a long time, a mixture of emotions warring in her. Last night it had seemed that she would have to go. Gradually a sense of relief crept in. She had not wanted to walk out on this job and let Louis down. Neither did she wish to be dismissed. And yet she had known they could not endure working together. She felt a sense of gratitude toward him for having made the decision to leave.

She went through the villa and opened the front door. The sun was not very high in the sky. The air was still with that particular early-morning stillness when no one else is awake. A terrible sense of desolation swept over her. She had a feeling of being alone in the world. More alone even than when Fay had died. Or before that, when her parents had gone. With a heartfelt sigh she returned to the kitchen for the basket and started off down the hill to the bakery. A tiny donkey pulling a cart met her plodding on its way, an old woman in black with a head scarf following behind. Shutters were being thrown open to the morning. Middle-aged women carrying baskets like hers emerged from side streets, hurrying, their shoes clattering on the cobblestones. And yet the familiar liveliness of early-morning Greece that she had loved no longer struck a spark in her. The whole place seemed without heart this morning. Even Stavros the baker did not seem his usual self. There was no gay, tempestuous greeting. Or perhaps today she was without the ability to sense happiness.

"Hello, Stavros."

"Hello, mees. I have your rolls ready." The Greek piled them into her basket and she left.

Back at the villa the guests were stirring. Astonishingly, Janine was setting the tables on the terrace. She wore the neat trousers and shirt she had put on the night before. Her feet were bare. She looked subdued. "Louis is gone." So she had had a note, too, Rosalie thought cynically. "I looked in his room. The bed was made up and his suitcase gone. What happened?"

Rosalie replied, "He had to return to London."

"So suddenly? Why?"

Rosalie shrugged. "Business, perhaps."

"He must have made a phone call. He disappeared rather suddenly after dinner last night."

"I expect so."

Janine heaved a sigh of regret. "Oh, well. Shall I put the coffee on?" She did not hear Rosalie's answer because she was engrossed in attracting the attention of a male guest who was coming up the path. Rosalie went to put the coffee on herself.

The days dragged by, endlessly. Janine, refusing to take any responsibility, added to the strain. "Louis told me you're the boss," she told Rosalie airily. "I'm to take orders." Now that Louis had gone she flirted with the male guests, changing her clothes at least three times a day. But she did work willingly enough when Rosalie directed her.

Stephen complained that he saw too little of Rosalie. "I'm busy," she told him. "You must see how busy I am."

"Nico is taking us to Naxos tomorrow."

"Yes." She allowed herself a wry smile. Did Stephen think these trips occurred spontaneously? Did he not realize she arranged them, searching the tavernas for the elusive Nicholas, ordering the food and wine for a picnic lunch, packing it all?

"You're coming, I hope. It would be nice for us to have a day together without these 'responsibilities' you talk about," he said resentfully. "It hasn't been very successful, has it? First there was Alexander, and now he's gone you're never around. I've only got

174

three days left and my holiday is over. I've got to go back."

"I am around," she demurred, "being busy. I try to do my work without it appearing too obvious. No, I'm not going to Naxos tomorrow, Stephen. My work ends when I see you all aboard the caïque. Janine will be in charge of operations. I'm tired. I'm going to have a quiet day on the beach by myself. I've got a great deal to do when you go. I've only one day to get the villas done over and prepared for the next lot of guests."

"A quiet day!" he echoed. "If you go to the beach alone you know what will happen. You'll be pestered out of your mind by Greek Romeos." As if she did not know! Her heart sank at the reminder. "I will come with you and look after you," Stephen announced firmly.

She found herself tugged a little both ways, irritated by his persistence, yet knowing he spoke the truth. "You would enjoy Naxos. You must see it." But she spoke halfheartedly. It was true she was tired. And too dispirited to care. Perhaps his company would be good for her. She smiled kindly at him. "All right. You win."

Stephen was beside himself with excitement. He sang around the villa that evening while the guests were changing for dinner, pouring apéritifs on the terrace, chatting.

"He's terribly in love with you," Janine said conversationally as they washed up some glasses together. "And you're in love with Louis, aren't you?" It was a statement rather than a question. Rosalie ignored it. "The trouble is," Janine confided, "Louis is still in love with a dream, so you may as well forget him until he gets over the other girl. She treated him abominably and he's still bruised."

175

Rosalie stiffened. "He told you that? Some girl treated him abominably?"

"She was a devil," Janine went on artlessly, wiping a glass and setting it upon a shelf above her head. "You don't mind my wearing these high heels tonight, and the jump suit, do you?" she asked apologetically. "I do like Quentin and he doesn't take any notice of me. There are only three days left, and I would like to see him again. So I thought, if you don't mind my dressing up—"

"Tell me about this devil," said Rosalie, choking, scarcely having heard a word the other girl said. "What did Louis tell you?"

"Oh, her." Janine racked her brains. "He said she was pretending to love him and all the time she was sleeping with another man. And suddenly he realized she was pregnant."

"With his child! *His* child," said Rosalie in a frozen voice.

"No. Apparently not. He hadn't been to bed with her. Apparently she was a virginal kind of girl—or so he thought. He was madly in love and he wanted to marry her. What's the matter, Rosalie? Why are you looking at me like that?"

"Because I knew that girl," said Rosalie, her voice low with fury. "It's true, as he said, that she was a virginal kind of girl. But that's all the truth in his terrible story. He's abominable. A despicable liar. He violated her. She was having his child and he—he—he threw her out."

Janine stared at Rosalie in astonishment. "I thought you were in love with him. Why, you're crying. I'm sorry, Rosalie, I'm terribly sorry. I shouldn't be talking about this. I'd no idea."

Rosalie dashed the tears from her eyes and, pulling herself together, said sadly, "I'm sorry, too. I didn't want to talk about it, either. But I couldn't help . . . I—I—I hate him so."

Janine looked at her with a compassion Rosalie would never have guessed she possessed. She said only, "You're crying again," and handed Rosalie a tissue.

"Come on. It's time we left for Spiro's."

Chapter Twelve

It was the same as all the other picnic days. Rosalie rose early and went off to the bakery because it was easier to do that herself than haul Janine out of bed and listen to her yawns and early-morning complaints. She packed the lunch basket and together the two girls made breakfast. The guests were happy this morning. They loved going out in the caïque. There were raised eyebrows and knowing looks when they heard that neither Rosalie nor Stephen was going along. But the holiday was nearly over. Their smiles said they understood Stephen was making a last-ditch effort to win back his lost love. And they all conceded volubly that Rosalie deserved a day off.

"You're too kind," she murmured.

"You do too much for us." They knew, compassionately, that she was overworked, often doing Janine's work as well as her own.

"You appreciate it, so I don't mind," she said with a smile. She knew they planned to buy a present for her. She had come across groups whispering surreptitiously in corners.

She and Stephen saw them off from the quay. She never quite felt she could totally rely on Nicholas, Spiro's black-eyed, wily, charming cousin. She had to satisfy herself that he had turned up. They waved the party away, watching while the caïque putt-putted out beyond the breakwater; then they turned to walk along the cobblestoned quay past the idling caïques, the pelicans, and the tourists toward the square where buses waited. Rosalie wore her yellow bikini beneath a thin cotton dress she had bought in one of the little boutiques. It was gathered at the shoulders, then swung free across her small breasts and hips. One did not need underwear, for the hot Greek sun would dry a bikini in no time at all. And she had bought a shadier hat. They had not packed food. Stephen insisted he would take her to lunch at the beach café.

They found two seats in the bus. When it filled to overflowing, with passengers packed like sardines inside and an overflow hanging on at the steps, the driver started the engine. They ground off up the hill, past the three white villas looking pretty in front of the picturesque windmill; past the little white cubes of houses, the chapels with their barred windows and high crosses; past market gardens and drowsing donkeys in poppy-laden fields; then with a labored roar from the engine they went over the top and came rattling down the long slope to the magnificent golden beach. Stephen was kind and attentive, helping Rosalie down, carrying her towel. They walked across the sand, shed their brief outer garments, and went directly into the calm blue sea. Rosalie swam out a hundred yards, then turned to float on her back. A moment later Stephen came up beside her, puffing. "My! You swim well," he gasped. "I couldn't have gone another inch."

"You shouldn't have come out so far," she cried, alarmed. "Turn over and float." He did so, obedient as a child. "Keep your head down or you'll sink. Stretch out your arms. Stiffly. Stiffly, Stephen." He did as she said and with a pang Rosalie remembered how Louis and she had come here, cutting through the water like seals, pushing each other under with careless rapture, bobbing up laughing. She thrust the disturbing memory out of her mind, turned on her back again, and floated with Stephen until he was sufficiently rested. Then they swam slowly back to the shore.

"Sorry about that," he said ruefully. "I didn't know you were such a good swimmer." She nearly said he didn't know much about her at all. Theirs had been a very brief love affair before he went off with Fay. She had not seen him again until the funeral.

They had lunch under the awning as she and Louis had done. "Lobster," he said, holding out the menu, smiling at her. "Let's have lobster, and a bottle of Demestica."

She swallowed over a lump in her throat. "Not lobster," she said, the words coming unbidden. She could not have eaten the same meal she had with Louis, if her life depended on it.

"I thought you liked lobster." Stephen frowned. "I heard you say—"

She cut in brusquely, hating herself but unable to stop, "Not today, Stephen. It's very filling. And I'm not that hungry. Some kind of fish. And not Demestica. I had it one night and—and—"

"And what?" He looked at her curiously.

"I talked too much," she replied lamely, looking away, blinking against a mist that was coming up behind her eyes.

He laughed. "Is that all? I'd like you to talk too much. Let's have Demestica," he said happily, raising one hand to signal to the waiter.

"*No.*" She felt her face go hard, the muscles tightening beyond her control. "No," she said bleakly. "If we must have wine, let's have retsina. It's the local drink. It's what everyone else has."

"I wanted this lunch to be special. You're spoiling it," he complained.

"I'm sorry." But that was all she could say.

Later, they lay on the beach in the boiling sun. A couple close by were in each other's arms, kissing. Rosalie glanced at them, then looked away. "It's the heat," commented Stephen, amused. He leaned upon his elbows, looking down into Rosalie's face. "The heat gets at me, too." She gazed at him without feeling. There was numbness inside. His head came down and he kissed her on the lips. There was no instinctive response, even male to female. Nothing.

She pushed herself upright. "Let's go for a walk." They left the beach and walked at a steady pace along a grass-bordered, dusty track. Ahead was a clump of trees, and beyond that, another. The beach curved around to a point. They followed its line.

Eventually Stephen spoke. "You're in love with Alexander, aren't you?"

Her head came up and she looked at him stonily. "I hate him. I have never detested anyone as much in my whole life. Louis is dishonest, cruel, totally without scruples."

Stephen's mouth fell open. For a full moment he

181

seemed unable to reply. Then he said quietly, "Fay told you it was his child, didn't she?"

It was Rosalie's turn to be dumbfounded. "You knew? You knew all the time Louis was father of her child?"

"No, because Louis was not the father," Stephen replied in a strained voice. "Didn't you know about Fay?"

"Know?" she echoed, a pain going right through the heart of her.

"Fay was— I'm going to tell you this, Rosalie, because I think you need to know. I'm sorry because it's going to hurt you badly. Get ready for it. Fay loved only one person—herself." In the silence that followed his words Stephen eyed her curiously. "You did know," he said. "I can see. It isn't a bombshell, after all. But you wouldn't accept it. You couldn't face it."

"No," Rosalie's reply was a mere whisper on the wind.

"She was promiscuous," Stephen went on. "I'm not going into details. It's all over and I don't want to upset you. You knew Fay's angel face could capture any man. Louis Alexander. Me. Any man she ever met. She could get them if she wanted them, and she couldn't resist the power she had. She was self-indulgent in the extreme. Only Louis was strong enough to throw her out when he found she was pregnant.

"I fell for her wiles the second time," he went on bitterly, "even though she had ditched me once. I couldn't believe my luck—until I found out the truth. Even after we were married she continued to see one of her lovers." He stopped and turned Rosalie to face him. "You've got to believe what I say. Louis won't tell you. He's too honorable, I daresay. But she did a terrible thing to me, and I don't mind speaking out now—for your sake. Because I love you, Rosalie. I think I always loved you, but I blew it by going to pieces over Fay."

"She died," Rosalie said in a choked voice, making a last-ditch attempt to save the memory of the girl she had loved.

"You can will yourself to die, if you hate yourself enough and don't want your baby, and . . . I don't know," Stephen said bitterly. "It would take a psychiatrist to explain, and maybe he couldn't. Fay didn't want to live, in the end. Don't cry, Rosalie. Or, all right, do," he amended, offering his shoulder. "Just one more time. I'm glad I've been able to do that much for you. Make you face up to the truth at last. It will be easier now for you to accept Fay's death." After a while he said sadly, "I'm sorry you can't love me. But I do understand. He's a good fellow, Louis. Your grandmother told me he forgave Fay in the end. He put a posy on her grave with a card saying he forgave her. That's more than I would do."

"I know," she admitted. "I didn't want to face the truth."

Rosalie went to the tiny airfield to welcome the new arrivals. It was another glorious, cloudless Greek day, with the tiny islands of the Cyclades butting up out of the sapphire ocean like little brown mice and the white, so white cubes of Mykonian houses glittering in the clear air. She stood at the edge of the tarmac waiting, dressed prettily in a soft little embroidered sun dress from the best boutique in town, her hair shining in a golden halo around her head, the tendrils lifting on the wind, her eyes alight with excitement. As the plane landed she felt the blood throbbing wildly in her veins. She glanced down as she had done a dozen times at the telegram clutched in her hand.

ARRIVING WITH GUESTS STOP   THANKS TO STEPHEN
STOP   LOVE AND LOVE AND MORE LOVE
STOP   LOUIS

She watched with an almost unbearable longing as he came down the steps from the aircraft. He was half a head taller than anyone else, his shoulders more square, his chin high, a vibrant male creature glorying in his strength and vitality. He was wearing an impeccably cut summer suit, the shirt open to reveal the dark tan of his neck and chest.

Her heart swelled until it was ready to burst. She turned and went back to the gate where they would exit. Her knees were trembling. The passengers came through with their luggage, a laughing, happy group, excited as the first lot had been, pale-skinned as she and Louis were not, friendly, expecting fun. She smiled tentatively at them. "I'm Rosalie. Come with me." She could not see Louis. She guessed he was deliberately staying behind. Their meeting had to be—not private, for that was impossible—but as private as they could make it. She bundled the guests into the waiting bus.

"Where's Mr. Alexander?" someone asked. "And what about you?"

"We'll be following."

"There's plenty of room."

"Don't worry." The bus driver started the engine and the vehicle lumbered off. She turned. And now Louis was there, standing alone in the doorway. She ran and he ran. They met somewhere halfway. Their arms came around each other. She was crying too hard to speak, remembering the loneliness of the days since he left, the hopelessness when she thought they could never come together.

"Darling, I love you."

"I've always loved you. From the first moment."

"From the first moment," he repeated in a voice that told her he could scarcely believe his luck.

She turned, somewhat ruefully indicating the concrete mixer's little truck. "We've got our own transport. Angelo said I could borrow it while he had his siesta. Only till five o'clock. I didn't want a taxi driver looking on."

Louis glanced at his watch and those lion eyes glimmered. They laughed softly together, visualizing their two hours' respite while Janine settled the guests in.

They slid together into the truck and Louis started the engine. "There's a little woody inlet on a side road," she began tentatively. "I found it on the way. It's not much of a road, but . . ." There had to be a secret trysting place for their first real coming together. Her voice was drowned by the revving of the engine. They dashed along, the spinning of the wheels matching the fast beating of their hearts. It seemed only a broken moment before they were diving down the side road into the secret bay.

Louis braked and switched off the engine, and they jumped out. There was the inlet with the white waves murmuring among the rocks. A group of trees, craggy, windswept, and romantic, hovered at the edge of the sand. They stood there, two beautiful people, arms entwined, torn by primitive passions that matched the wild landscape. Below them great rocks jutted up on either side of a strip of sand, making a tiny room with the sky its ceiling, the water its door, and the trees above rendering fickle shade. They stepped down onto the beach. "There's so much to say," said Louis, gazing down into her upturned glowing face. "But first, the most important question. Will you do me the honor—"

"Of course I will. Of course I will. Could you doubt it?" She laughed like a child. "It has been so awful, trying not to love you."

"That's one thing at which you were inefficient, thank heavens."

They sat down beside the sun-hot rocks. "We've got to talk about Fay," Louis said soberly.

"Yes."

"The bad part. And then, never again," said Louis. "You loved her, and so did I. But we can only remember her with love after we've said it all out loud. You saw that card, *Forgiveness,* on her grave." It was a statement rather than a question. Rosalie nodded. "What else could I put? Not, 'I forgive you for what you did to me.' For that was what I meant, darling."

Again, Rosalie nodded. "Perhaps I knew, but I wouldn't allow myself to accept it. She treated you badly, I know. She was looking for a father for her child."

"I never slept with her," said Louis. "I realize this may sound odd, knowing what you know about Fay now, but she was so apparently . . . virginal."

Rosalie nodded again. "It was the look she had."

"And we were going to get married immediately. I'd never felt that way about any girl. I'd never wanted to marry any girl before. She was a sort of fairy princess. A bit of Dresden china. I put her on a pedestal. After all, I wasn't going to have to wait long. Then I learned the awful truth about her promiscuousness. Somebody spilled the beans to me, and I confronted her. She didn't say a word in her own defense. She didn't attempt to deny it. She simply got out of her chair, walked through the door, and that was the end. I never saw her again. And I swear to you, darling, I didn't know she was pregnant. Please believe me."

"Of course I do."

"It was agony. I had gone right overboard for the first time in my life. I used to wake up in the night thinking it was all a bad dream. I even got my friend to introduce me to one of the crowd she had been getting around with. It was so difficult to believe the truth."

"Don't torture yourself," said Rosalie. "It's all over. And now . . ." She put a finger gently across his lips, sealing them. "We agreed never to speak of her again without affection. You met her during a bad stage in her life. I've accepted it, and you've forgiven her. What more is there to say?"

"Can one get married on a Greek island?"

"Why not? Let's try."

His arms tightened. The Greek sun shone down on them. "Aphrodite, goddess of love, will be at our wedding. Could there possibly be a better beginning?"

4 FREE BOOKS

See coupon
on reverse panel.

Silhouette Romance

Few authors have the unique ability to capture the spirit of truly satisfying romance. And of those who do, most are writing for Silhouette. Included within this constellation of star writers, you'll find . . .

- ✔ **Janet Dailey**
- ✔ **Anne Hampson**
- ✔ **Brooke Hastings**
- ✔ **Patti Beckman**
- ✔ **Elizabeth Hunter**
- ✔ **Mary Carroll**

Enjoy the enchanting craftsmanship of all our multi-talented writers as a member of the Silhouette Book Club.

Start with the set of 4 Silhouette Romances listed. They're *yours to keep FREE even if you never buy another book.*

Then let us arrange for you to receive a complete set of six new Silhouette Romances every month. You'll get them days before they go on sale anywhere.

And we pay all postage and handling costs. You may cancel anytime you choose.

RIA

Receive These 4 Books Free!

Free-Books Certificate

MAIL TODAY To Reserve Your Home Subscription

Silhouette BOOK CLUB OF CANADA

P.O. Box 910, Stratford, Ontario N5A 6W3

YES, please send me FREE, and without obligation, the 4 exciting Silhouette paperback originals listed above. Unless you hear from me after I receive my 4 FREE BOOKS, please send me 6 full-length, Silhouette Romances to preview each month, as soon as they are published. I understand that you will bill me just $1.75 each (a total of $10.50) with *no additional shipping, handling or other hidden charges.* There is no minimum number of books that I must buy, and I can cancel this arrangement anytime I wish. The first 4 books are mine to keep, even if I never take a single additional book.

Signature _____
(If under 18, parent or guardian must sign)

Name _____

Address _____

City _____

Prov. _____ Postal Code _____

4 FREE BOOKS NOW . . .
6 BOOKS DELIVERED RIGHT
TO YOUR HOME!

This offer limited to one per household, expires May 31, 1983. If price changes are necessary after that date, you will be notified.

RtB

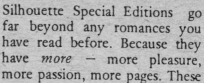

SILHOUETTE SPECIAL EDITIONS

Silhouette Special Editions go far beyond any romances you have read before. Because they have *more* — more pleasure, more passion, more pages. These are big, powerful stories that will fire your imagination. You'll meet ardent lovers — thrill to exciting conflict and drama — share intimate moments of tender passion. Silhouette Special Editions keep you entranced as you turn each page.

4 Silhouette Special Editions FREE — no strings attached

Now you can get the first four Silhouette Special Editions ever published, absolutely *free*. "Terms of Surrender" . . . "Intimate Strangers" . . . "Mexican Rhapsody" . . . "Valaquez Bride." A $7.80 value, *yours free*, if you act now.

We believe you will be thrilled with your four books, and will want to receive Silhouette Special Editions regularly through our home subscription service. Every month we will send you six new books just as soon as they are published. Look them over for 15 days. Silhouette Special Editions are delivered right to your door with never a charge for postage or handling — and there's no obligation to buy anything at any time.

READERS' COMMENTS ON SILHOUETTE ROMANCES:

"I would like to congratulate you on the most wonderful books I've had the pleasure of reading. They are a tremendous joy to those of us who have yet to meet the man of our dreams. From reading your books I quite truly believe that he will someday appear before me like a prince!"

—L.L.*, Hollandale, MS

"Your books are great, wholesome fiction, always with an upbeat, happy ending. Thank you."

—M.D., Massena, NY

"My boyfriend always teases me about Silhouette Books. He asks me, how's my love life and naturally I say terrific, but I tell him that there is always room for a little more romance from Silhouette."

—F.N., Ontario, Canada

"I would like to sincerely express my gratitude to you and your staff for bringing the pleasure of your publications to my attention. Your books are well written, mature and very contemporary."

—D.D., Staten Island, NY

*names available on request